HOW I KILLED YOU

K. I. GUIHER

NOTEBOOK

PUBLISHING

First published in 2020 by Notebook Publishing,
20–22 Wenlock Road, London, N1 7GU.

www.notebookpublishing.co

ISBN: 9781-913206512

A CIP catalogue record for this book is available from the British Library.

Typeset by Notebook Publishing.

I carry you with me, still.

Your ashes and dust nourish all beautiful things growing from the Earth.

CHAPTER 1:

THE SEA OF HEARTBREAK

I watched your taillights flash when you reached the bottom of our driveway. My heart leapt because I thought perhaps you were returning. Even if you were returning just for a moment to tell me what an ass I'd been, I would have welcomed it— and you would have been justified. Your right blinker flashed, you pulled out onto the road, and were gone.

The day was dark and dreary, and the rainy sadness swallowed your car. I only ever saw it once more, but you were not in it then. Pieces of you remained, but there was no life in them.

I strained my eyes. They had not yet started to cry. I squinted and wished as hard as I could that I could summon you back with my mind. When my thoughts were not able to bring you to me, I was alone with them. Haunted dreams came to me like a Dickens holiday tale. Sadly, the ghosts of broken hearts past and present were too late to save the souls of the future. A single tear breached my eyelid and began its slow journey down my face to hang from my chin. I did not wipe it away. Instead, I savored it until it fell on its own. The teardrop splatted on the hardwood floor in front of my toes, and I watched it there. The tear remained in a sad little drop, beaded up, and it would either be wiped away by my sock in an instant or stay there to evaporate. The slow death of a teardrop was more sorrow than I was able to bear, and I wiped it with my toe. Then it was gone, just as you were. Gone.

I forced myself to back away from the window. It was like fighting gravity because my heart wanted me to remain there and wait for you to return. I hesitated, because backing away—abandoning my post at the glass—would mean I accepted your departure. I felt there was a chance that all wasn't lost as long as I was still looking at the spot where I last saw you.

Your red taillight glow still lingered at the edge of the driveway like the leftover light in one's eyes after a camera flash. The heat of instant regret appeared and rose from deep inside. Lava scorched me as it followed my chakras up through my body to the center of my forehead, where it is said the "third eye" resides. It seared my insides, and I could physically feel the vibrations traveling through me, making me feel as if I might faint. My vision became less sharp, the room grew unnaturally dark, and I struggled to hold back a sob. The glob of the cry choked me, too large to swallow, and I was too fearful of allowing it to escape. What would the sound do to the remnants of my breaking heart? Would the spiteful monster living in the shadows of my spirit hear it and awaken again to cause further torment?

The dense, thick pain—the kind that comes and goes in waves—had yet to reach its crescendo, but it was rising. I could feel just the beginning of panic starting to poach my insides, and I became scared. I almost hoped I would drown in the waves of anguish as they crashed over me. I was drenched with tears of regret as an unending stream poured from deep within. I didn't want to live knowing the last thing I would ever see of you was the sad expression on your kind face and the red tail lights of your car.

Your aftershave—citrusy, musky and masculine—still ambled about in the great room. The tingle of your fingertips brushing my shoulder on your way out lingered. I placed my hand where yours had touched just a moment ago. Closing my eyes, squeezing them tightly, I wanted to visualize every detail of your face for the fear I may never see it again.

Rumi said, "Look as long as you can at the friend you love, no matter whether that friend is moving away from you or coming back towards you." Moving away from me, you were- gone with the bustle of traffic and spatter of rain.

I began to wonder what ingredients were in sorrow that had allowed it to consume me so quickly. In a moment, I had realized, all hope can be devoured, and one is left with mere bones and nothing more. A massive black vest filled with regret denser than lead was weighing me down, pulling me under a sea filled with tears. Salty, sorrowful tears, wept by the owners of broken souls, washed over me, and my hair floated and swirled. As more tears filled the sea, a current was created, and it caused my body to bob and sway. It lifted my feet just a little off the bottom, and then pushed me back down. I was nearly weightless and utterly powerless, and so I submitted to where the troubled sea took me. Shattered hearts lined the floor of this ocean of despair like fragments of seashells battered against rocks. They would cut and stab if I stepped on them, drawing blood that would swirl in the water and attract predators with sharp, nasty teeth, stinging barbs and black souls. Perhaps the biting creatures were my kindred. My burdensome vest would not allow me to rise above the salty waves. The bitter taste of saline tears filled my mouth. I gagged, spat, and choked as I was denied the right to breathe. I struggled briefly, then had no choice but to submit.

On the floor of the ocean of agony, I did not drown. I was anchored to the bottom by a Serpent. It was dark, nearly black, but appeared to be more shadow than impermeable, as if made from the smoke of a burning forest. Its tentacles intertwined with my thoughts. Instead of trying to escape, I let them each take a turn, wrapping one another around me, through me and into the very essence that was me. Each tentacle had a razor-sharp hook on its end with barbs so it could not be pulled out once sunk into flesh. These tentacles sent a searing pain through my soul. I hoped for the kindness of death, but reasoned I did not deserve such a luxury. With no toed sock to wipe me away, I would have to evaporate slowly.

The fifth of the Ten Commandments tells us not to kill. I thought I was obeying; I hadn't struck, shot, or stabbed anyone to bring them to death. I didn't *want* to do harm. What they hadn't taught me at Sunday School was what the Serpent's tentacles were now teaching me—and what a painful lesson to learn. Words have the ability to kill. Even worse, they can allow a soul to live with the guilt of vocal homicide inflicted upon others, while fearing that death never will come to the offender. Speaking hurtful words forces one to live with regret that soon becomes tears, and they flow freely into the dense, salty sea. I began to fill that sea with my weepy eyes. Regret was out in front of all other feelings, and it blurred my vision until I cried, releasing them into the sea. Despair followed regret like a faithful companion. They had been traveling together for eternity, holding gnarled hands on their harsh journey intended to foster lament.

The unforgiving, righteous tentacles held my darkened, heavy soul on the floor of the sea of heartbreak. Weakened by sorrow as well as fright, I was unable to raise my head from the ocean's floor. The Serpent used Its tentacles to hold my eyes open and my head up. It insisted I watch the scene It was going to play for me. There was no kindness or mercy in Its touch. How I killed you in the most torturous and inhumane way a person can kill another; with words that can never be retrieved once allowed to escape. I murdered you slowly, one piece at a time. By killing you, I fed the monster that lived within me.

The first tentacle attached itself to my heart. I could feel the sharp barbs as it connected to me, and with every beat, they worked their way in deeper. It forced me to view the scene where everything began to change. Where I started to kill your precious soul. The essence of you that loved me so purely, so sweetly, and so tenderly.

We were still new. Happy days when we drank rain in the forest, inhaled warm sunshine and picked berries to nibble, but also made sure to save some for the bears—your idea, not mine. Generous, you were, even to the beasts that roamed the woods. Always with care for all living things and, most of all, for me. While walking, holding hands, and smelling the sweet decay of dropped leaves in the enchanted forest, I loved you so. Just touching you filled my heart with poetry. When we couldn't be together, I would comfort myself by thinking of you, and it would cause me to skip and sing. You were the first love story I had ever heard. You were the sweetest ballad ever played, and your song was just for me. How I wish my empty soul would have been healthier, devoid of the rabid virus that infected me. If it had been so, I could have taken better care of the treasure that you were. I could have enhanced your gifts and your life. With a proper love that wasn't killing you, you could have shone even more brightly than you already were.

We discovered the gentleness and fragility of love in my apartment, where we cuddled and laughed. So many evenings we had that were full of joy, love, and hope. New love is made of stardust and is pure magic. Oh, if that feeling were to never subside; if only it had been possible to bottle the excess in the beginning and save it for when the newness of love starts to wither. There is comfort in finding what you believe to be the match to your soul. A perfect fit to love and honor forever. A heart is never as light and airy as when love is new. The feeling that your beloved is walking beside you even when you are separated makes one never completely alone. The gentle sting of a tear is caused by pure joy, always ready to swell. It tickles, new love does. A sweet, light tickle that can be felt right behind one's heart. It flutters there and becomes intoxicating. The flutter travels up the neck and to the jaw. Hope is always present, and smiles come easily and naturally. The sweet butterfly of new love brushes its painted wings on everything inside. Butterflies are fragile and delicate beings, easily killed when mistreated. They must be handled with the gentlest of care and loved with the kindest of love. Be well aware! The wind caused by a harsh word is enough to begin killing the beautiful, fluttery being. Verbal assault rips off the little bug's wings; sends it spiraling to the floor of the sea of heartache among the fragmented souls previously thrown against the rocks, smashed and left to decay.

You kissed my lips so sweetly. You were always so gentle with my body, as well as my soul. Your light, soft touches, which were like a butterfly's wings, attested to how much you cherished me, and you were always careful not to harm my delicate self. When you ran your hand through my hair and down my back, a small spark of static gave us a tiny zap. Nearly dark in the room, the little blue arc of it quickly flashed as if we had made our very own small thunderstorm. What a fond memory that could have been. We could have laughed and joked about it for the ages, holding hands on our swing in the twilight years of our lives. We could have remembered the little storm we made with our love.

The spark surprised you, and you laughed. It startled me, and I began to kill you. Your laughter infuriated me. We were then still a shiny new couple. The stardust dreams were still alive, but the smallest ones had mere seconds left. I composed myself, climbed out of your lap, and walked away while I was still in control of my rage. I could feel the poison rising in me. I had been bitten long ago by something wicked, rabid, and unknown. I intended to infect you as well as anyone who became close to me. It rose through my soul and was *so* hot and hateful. That particular strain of venom was fast-acting, and there was not enough time for me to get the elixir. I needed anti-venom, not for me but for you. I knew that very soon I was going to use the poison I spat from my mouth to begin the killing.

You cared so much and loved me so profoundly that, of course, when I walked away, you followed me out of the room. A man like you would never wish for me to face alone whatever monster was climbing up through me. You were a knight. You gently touched my elbow with your sweet fingers, and that was it, the beast that lived inside of me sentenced you to death.

I spun around and spat white-hot hateful words at you. I wanted you hurt, blinded, and I wanted you dead. I meant to wound you so severely that you wouldn't be able to feel happiness again. You had the ability to laugh at the shock of the static. How could you when it was such a serious offense? Couldn't you see it was a personal attack on me? The words I said do not matter. The spirit I told them in, though...

Until that moment, you never thought it possible for me ever to treat you as anything but a treasure. Why would you? You completely trusted me to provide you with soft, sweet, gentle love. Of course you did. There was no reason to believe otherwise.

As the tentacle burned through my soul, I could still see the absolute horror on your face. The color drained from you, and your eyes looked down. I killed your innocent smile. You looked at the floor, backed away like you were about to be ripped apart by an evil, torturous creature; a beast that had transformed into a wicked thing with teeth and claws right before your eyes. A steely thing was coming for you with no forgiveness. It would grind a heart into dust without stalling. I gained immense power by your backing away. I fed on your retreat as a lion would feast on a deer. When you run from a predatory animal, they chase. With claws and fangs extended, I started for your jugular.

The look of shock on your sweet, kind face fulfilled a craving in me. It was as if I had blacked out and became possessed by an evil version of myself. I could feel my real being in there, way back where even my most profound thoughts could never be reached. I was not able to regain possession of my words and deeds. When fully satiated, the monster retreated from the front of my mind, and I grabbed you and kissed your precious face.

"I am so sorry, I don't know why I reacted that way," I told you and meant it. I cried. Not for attention or sympathy, but because I was sincerely mournful for killing you. I could not understand what made me react the way I did. I always knew something wicked was alive inside of me, but I never dreamed it would surface in your presence. Even after it subsided, I could still feel it squirming agitatedly behind my ribcage. It had a taste of power and was eager for another bite.

You made a little joke, and we laughed. I wiped my tears, and we moved forward with our evening. Our love was an infant that had to witness the killing of its givers of life. It was a mortal wound. All wounds are mortal to some degree, particularly the ones inflicted with words. Word wounds rip and tear, and can never fully heal because they cause too much damage. An injury from a sharp object can be sewn shut or left to scab over, but one from a word festers forever, lurking just beneath the surface. Everything changed that day. A line had been crossed, which can never be crossed back over. Once the hurtful stuff escapes, it is loose forever. It was a minor change, unnoticeable, really, but our love was never precisely the same; it was weakened and began slowly dying. If it were visible, one would have been able to see the heart crumbs starting to fall to the seafloor ever so slightly. They would drop like glitter, drifting to the bottom to collect with the others that had fallen before them.

As the scene faded and the tentacle burned, I came back to myself. I had returned to my newly empty home. It felt as though the scene went on for hours in a hallucination that had ebbed and flowed. The trail from the teardrop was still damp on my chin. My eyes were full now, brimming but not spilling. The tears were built up convexly and distorted my vision. I thought about you. I thought about how we would laugh and say silly things. I thought about how, when you kissed me, my lip would often get stuck just a little bit in between the two of yours as if you were trying to keep me there. I can still feel the little "plop" it made when it gently came away. I felt your breath in my hair when you walked behind my chair and kissed the top of my head. Your warm exhale allowed the scent of hair products and mint to cascade and waft all around my face. You always wanted to touch me. You would walk the long way around just so you could brush me with a gentle finger. I loved you so deeply, and you were such a unique soul.

Underneath my heart, back where the monster sometimes sent me, I ached for you. A closeness that wasn't entirely you had stalled inside me, buzzing, wanting to be free. I began once again to slip away into the black.

The Serpent wrapped a bladed tentacle around my throat. Its appendage was crusted with diamonds from rings given to symbolize promises of love and cherishing. When promises are fractured and tossed against the concrete walls we build to keep ourselves safe from the outside, the rings' crystals crumble. The debris from the stones of broken promises is gathered by the serpents and turned into slicing instruments meant to torture sweet, innocent lovebirds.

This tentacle was sharp, and I could feel how it wanted to slice into my flesh with the jagged diamond edges. Still, it wouldn't do me the kindness of ending the suffering of my life. I wasn't worthy of the peace that would inevitably follow the slicing of my slender neck. Instead, it held me underneath the billowing, damning sea.

The ocean was dense and heavy like chowder, but it was without the comfort of the loving hands that would prepare a proper soup for a family dinner. All of the weight of it was pushing down on me. The cumbersome abyss caused me to stumble and fall. I tried to look up, searching for light and a direction to swim, but I could only see the floating dead souls of others who had killed the adoration of their beloved just as I had. I could hear the distant moans of the damned and sorrowful souls all entangled forever in their watery tomb. Donte would have marveled at the magnificence of the rolling watery Hell in which we all were trapped, not permitted to drown. My neck ached from the tentacle's strength and the weight of tears that filled the sea. When I tried to move for some relief, comfort was denied. Instead, replayed for me, was the scene that depicted the next time I killed you.

We were so very young. The struggles of young couples trying to carve a path in the world are something that should be cherished and looked back upon with fondness. The simple pleasures; a dinner out with friends, a bottle of wine shared between the two young, financially struggling, sweethearts... These things meant so very much in the early years when dreams of homes and new vehicles were not even seriously considered. A couple that contains two healthy partners flourishes and grows a more robust bond from conquering the everyday problems of young struggles.

You worked so achingly hard; two jobs so that we could be secure. You labored until your fingers were swollen and your muscles sore. I wanted to become a writer, and you meant to see to it that my aspiration was brought to life. It seemed as though your dream was to fulfill mine. Such a strong, brave man you were, and you never once complained. You were so generous with your time. Your jobs kept you away for many long, tiresome hours, and you did it because you wanted to care for me. You wanted me to have all of the desires of my heart to become fulfilled. You wanted me to write. An unfortunate irony is that only now do I write about you.

I loved how you loved me and how you wanted me to be safe. And I *was* safe. It was you, my love, who was in danger.

You stopped with a friend to watch a baseball game after working two shifts every day for many, many days. You did so few things that didn't include me, and you adored baseball. Even listening to a game on the radio, you would cheer and shout. It was so endearing; listening as I sat in our garden, hearing you inside celebrating your favorite team. You were offered a ticket from your friend and called me excitedly to tell me you would be late. We had plans for the evening, but in your excitement you forgot. I didn't, however, and I decided that perhaps you should be killed. Hot blood started to rush to my face while raw hatred and anger coursed through me as I paced the house. Abhorrent thoughts played on a loop in my head for hours until you returned home. There were moments I thought I would be able to silence the beast and keep it caged. I wish I would have been able to protect you from it. You protected me from everything, but you couldn't save either one of us from the beast that dwelt in my empty, blackened soul. Thoughts of subduing the raging monster were always quickly shoved away. It was a powerful, dominant beast. My true self that loved you so dearly was inside still, but pushed to the back where I had to watch in a state of helplessness as I killed your essence.

You came home, and I wouldn't speak to you. I put you in such an unfair position, and my poison removed the joy you had experienced with your friend at the baseball game. I was jealous you had chosen baseball and a friend over me. How could you? I ignored you until you came into our room to defend yourself for going to a game. You didn't shout; you just wanted me to understand, because you didn't want me to be sad. I saw the worry on your face. I was glad to see it had replaced the smile you wore when you had arrived home. I wanted you to feel poorly. I wanted you to know what a shitty man you were. How could you leave me for a baseball game?

The tentacle held me down even harder as I watched myself start packing. I was leaving you because you weren't able to recognize the severity of your offense. You showed remorse, but there was not enough remorse in the world to make up for going to a baseball game after work. I packed my clothes, smashed a photograph of us on the first vacation we ever had. You followed me, and when I got to the door, you gently touched my elbow with your fingertips. You weren't the kind of man that wanted me to run off in an emotional state and put myself in danger. Why would you? You invested so much of your precious time protecting me and caring for me that, of course, you ran after me.

I would give every sight I have ever seen to be able to hold our vacation photograph one last time. I longed to view it once again. The picture captured your big smile and windswept hair, but it is gone, just like you.

My inner demon was once again dragging me into the darkness where I was frightened to go. I spun around in your face and screamed horrid names at you, and then I used my next weapon—a dagger.

"I hate you," I screamed, twisting those words into your heart. When I saw how badly I hurt you, I was pleased and once again fulfilled. You put your hands up to your face. You didn't want me to see your tears. Not because you were too tough to cry, but because you knew your tears eventually would hurt me worse if I were to actually see them. You protected me from everything, including my own dagger. I stared as you retreated into the house and sat on the floor. You were finally defeated—and I had once again bested you. The dagger stopped twisting in my hand, and I dropped the bags I was carrying.

I stepped over you and went to bed, leaving you alone with the pain you deserved. I was still too emotional to sleep, so I went back to where you sat, unmoved from where I left you.

"I'm *sorry*," I said softly, brushing your cheek with my hand.

You were no longer able to protect me from seeing your tears. They flowed, a deluge of tears, and you couldn't speak.

I cried for what I had done. My cry was an honest one—I hated that I had hurt you. "I don't know why, my love... I just don't know why," I said when you asked me for an explanation. And it was the truth for I *didn't* know why and I *didn't* realize it wasn't healthy to have a monster living inside. The beast had lived in me for as far back as my memory stretched; it seemed almost natural. It was a horror-inducing thing with the power to push my true self back into a corner, helplessly watching as the killing began.

The only words you could choke out were, "Please don't hate me. I love you so very much." Even the Serpent cried when those were spoken.

"I am *so* sorry," I whispered again. I was sincere. I wished I hadn't killed you, but I had.

For many days after this daggering, the change in you and our love was noticeable. You didn't smile. You'd always had your breakfast sitting beside me, our knees touching. It was the way we had always eaten our breakfast every day since the first time we were together in the morning. *Touching knees*, we called it, but no more. Now you ate alone at the table. There was no joy in the Pop-Tarts you used to love to munch on; around the crusts first, saving the middle for last and always offering me a taste. We repaired things, and after a little while it was hardly noticeable anymore. However, we never again sat at breakfast touching knees. That part of our love was cold, breathless, and destined to decay. I killed it. Smashed it against the rocks, watching it shatter into diamond dust.

Mourning isn't a strong enough word to describe the emotions I felt at the loss of our touching knees. Sometimes I still lean my knee against something reliable and steady at breakfast and pretend it's you. Your unfinished box of Pop-Tarts sits in our cabinet, still hoping for your return. I see them and want to explain, but I cannot admit my ghastly behavior to your cheery breakfast treat. Often, I cradle your still-unwashed coffee cup near my heart and sing dirges to it until I hear it weep.

The scene faded to dark, and I was still in our empty home. Tears that were brimming had fallen and were wet on my socks and the floor in front of me. My nose began to run, and a squeak escaped from my throat as I tried to hold back a cry. I went to our kitchen for a towel and a sip of water. My mouth was so dry. I could feel the jittery feeling that crawls up from one's sternum towards the throat when things are about to get rough. I sobbed. I was so sorry for killing you.

I cried while I wobbled my way to the bedroom. *Should I lie down here?* It is so odd the way a room changes when there is somebody never coming back to it. All the furnishings were the same, as were the wall hangings. Different, foreign and unbearable was that room, and I couldn't stay in there. I went back to the kitchen, sat at the table, and lay my head on my arms. I looked around the room. It seemed so dark, even though the usual lights were on and shining.

The ice cubes dropped from the maker in the freezer. I remember how excited you were at that pure pleasure when we bought it. You beamed with joy when we brought it home. "Ice any time we want it," you kept saying. Your love of the simple things made my heart swell with a strong passion for you, but I killed you anyway.

The dagger that was held by the tentacle was lying forgotten on the seafloor. It was done with me, and I started to try to swim back to the surface when a violent shock pulled me down. A third tentacle tugged at me and attached to my chest, wrapping around and zapping me like a live wire. I tried to pry It from me, but when I did, It played a scene I wished would leave me because that scene was just too hard to bear. Harder still to endure was the fact I was sure it was not the worst scene to come if they were all going to be played out before I drowned. This scene was merely one of the many times I had killed you. I marvel at how natural killing becomes when done regularly. It becomes impossible for one to gauge the depth of their cuts when cutting is commonplace.

I was in our yard when you came home early from work—a surprise, and a pleasant one. I jogged to the car to greet you, excited to have you home so soon, but you didn't look well.

"What's the matter, my sweet love?" I asked.

We took you to the hospital, where tests were done. The results were very, very bad. We looked at x-rays and pictures, talked about plans on how to win and what to do if we couldn't. I was numb, and you comforted me. *You* comforted *me*. Why wouldn't you? You'd spent your life protecting me from so many dangerous, scary things. We went home, and I was making dinner when you suggested we go away. Your idea angered me. I launched into a tirade.

"Go away? How can we go away? How can you not take this seriously?" I scolded and tried to shame you. During the most terrifying moment of your life, I could only think of myself.

I walked away and went to the back yard to be in our garden. You followed me because you couldn't bear the thought of me out there alone and scared. I was your precious love, and you continued to care for me when you really needed to care for yourself. I turned my back to you when I saw you coming across the lawn. You touched my elbow gently with your fingers. You wanted to assure me we would do whatever was the most comfortable for me. Even at your darkest hour, I was your first concern. If only you had met someone before you met me. If I could have made a wish for you, it would have been that.

I spun around and shook your fingers away from me. "Don't fucking touch me," I screamed in your face. *I screamed in your face.*

Venomous spittle flew from my raging mouth. You stepped back away from me, but continued to try to explain. Again, you said you wanted us to go away together for just a short trip. I knew you thought it would probably be the last one you ever went on. How could I ever go away with you, knowing that when we returned home we would never go away again? I would have spent every moment recognizing it was the last time. I would be sad. My concern was that *I* would be sad. I turned away from you again, and again you brushed my elbow with your gentle fingers. I spun around on you once more and screamed hateful words directly into your wounded, worried face.

"Yes, let us go away, so when you *die* I can be stuck with that trip in my head. Just die now and we can be done with this stupidity," I seethed—and so hatefully at you. The evil creature that had taken up residence in my soul had no mercy. How could such a monster dwell in one who *is* capable of feeling love?

Your already worried face dropped so hard. I watched it melt, slowly, almost dripping off you. You were the strongest man I ever knew, but those words punched you so hard you literally staggered backward and fell. Your mouth opened in a scream that had no sound, and your face contorted in excruciation. I was glad to see I was getting through to you.

I felt guilty while I watched how hard you were fighting for a single breath. The terrible twisted state of your face was suffocating you. Finally, you pulled in air and were able to wail so hard that birds in a nearby tree took flight in favor of a more peaceful environment. Your breath gushed from you, then you gasped and wailed, and rocked yourself back and forth, hugging your knees. Entirely alone on the ground in our yard, you rolled, your shirt soaked with your tears. I killed you right there; shocked you to death.

"I don't want to die," you sobbed, "only because I don't want there ever to be a final day with you." Your head was down, and my fire destroyed you. "I can't believe you want me to die when I just want to be alive so I can be near you." Your precious face was soaked with tears and sweat. Your breath became labored and raspy, not from the cancer growing inside of you, but for the cancerous monster to which you pledged your love. I was the tumor that needed to be radiated. I was the killing disease. I wished for a scalpel to cut out the nasty mass that was my heart.

"I am so sorry," I said, and knelt beside you. I put my hand on your shoulder, and you shrugged it off. Never before had you shrugged away from my touch. "I am so *very* sorry, and I'm *scared*." I cried. I was sincere and ashamed. I stood up to leave you alone in the yard with your grief and the pain I had inflicted upon you. I let the killing blow take its course and crumble your heart into sea sand. When I got to my feet, you pulled at my hand. I helped you up, and we went inside. Once inside, you sat in your favorite chair. Alone in the dark, I could still hear you weep and shake. You spent the night there. When I awoke, you had already gone off to work.

Never before had you left our home for even a moment without telling me goodbye.

You recovered from the cancer growing in you, but I killed you that day, and from that you never really fully recovered. We salvaged some of our love, though, and went away as you had wished. You were distant with me after that and remained distant until you were gone. You were always kind and loving, but you had to become distant for your protection. Less twinkle in your eyes and less sparkle in your smile were the only remaining symptoms from your illness- *me.* Much of your playful humor came back, but much else of you was lost. You were so much more than that before I killed you.

Turning a passionate, caring soul into a distant being is the magic a monster brings. Evil survives by feeding on the good in those who are loved by the person it inhabits. Those who love deeply are most susceptible to being poisoned by fangs that drip hateful words.

The horror of that scene faded away, and I regained enough clarity to know that I was back, alone in the comfy house I shared with you. I stood up from the table and looked for a distraction. Outdoors in the dark, I found one. The little bunny you whittled out of wood for me was still on the stoop where you placed it so long ago, weathered and unmoved. How we used to joke and laugh about how poorly crafted it was. You were so many things, but a sculptor was not one. You did it as a lark because you wanted to make me laugh. I loved and adored it and its silliness. I left it on the step so that it was seen every time we entered our home and named it "Bun Bun." Oh, how I loved you. The Bunny sat there staring at me as I tried to compose myself. We shared a glance, and I had to look away. I could feel its gaze follow me and burn into my turned back. The Bunny came from your heart, and it hated me now because I had killed you. Bun Bun and I shared that sentiment.

Alone, under the dark sea of heartbreak and agony, the tentacle that was wrapped around my chest loosened and fell away. I started to swim towards the light, which was unreachably far above me, when yet another limb noosed around my neck, teasing to cut my life supply. I gasped, and then a scene unfolded in front of me. It was time, my love, time for the killing beast to step, once again, to the front.

Our anniversary, what a joyous occasion. Chemicals had devoured your cancer and spat it out. Healed! Heaven gave us all of the joy and relief of the world, but it fades away after the threat is gone. How easily our eager spiteful selves make their way back to us when there is no imminent danger. Just as it would be beneficial to bottle new love, bottling the relief of avoiding impending doom would be a valuable essence to save. In times when one is about to lose the battle with demons that dwell within, a capful of absolution would have healing properties to rival chemotherapy. A small dose of the relief felt when desperation vanished could cure many ills.

Could it kill the devil-like terror that raises its head to spit fiery hatred? Sadly, that is a question that will remain unanswered.

We celebrated with our friends; drinking, dancing, and being in love. Our limousine hit a small bump just as you were raising your glass in a toast to our friends. A splash plopped out onto my knee, and everyone laughed. They were laughing at me, and I had no choice: I decided I was going to kill you. I sat silently, not smiling or laughing while the three of you enjoyed the buzz of champagne and the buzz of friendship and love. A quiet rage built in me while the sounds of joy pierced my ears and my spiteful soul. As the sounds of pleasure became deafening, my monster became more awakened. When we reached our spot, our lovely friends were all waiting there to celebrate with us. I couldn't celebrate because I had killing to do. The wages of splashing and laughing were death.

I walked in with you and allowed you to hold my hand. At our table, you told your silly jokes, and everyone booed you just as always. You told them so you could entice the boos out of the crowd. How they loved you; the joy and laughter you provided made perfect strangers want to be near. They hung onto your every word, laughing and teasing. I couldn't listen to it, and so I got up without speaking and went out onto the street. Waiving down a taxi cab, I went home without a sound. An hour later, you arrived behind me. You weren't upset. You were only concerned about finding me in tears in a ball on the sofa. You gently brushed my elbow with your sweet fingers and asked me what happened. Of course you did, you were so caring and kind. The caress of your touch almost kept the monster away. I felt for a mere second that I would be able to push it back. Alas, it was more durable than I, and it clawed its way to the surface.

I rose from my ball on the sofa and spat hatred at you. My words were incoherent and intended to stab at your heart, but you weren't so easy to break anymore. You had grown weary of my attempts to kill you. You ran your hand through your hair, put your head down, and went to bed without a word. I immediately followed you into our room, continuing to try to envenomate your precious self. You grabbed me in an embrace, holding me tightly. You said you loved me, and then told me you were leaving. You brushed my hair out of my eyes, put clothes in a bag, and were gone.

I tasted then just a hint of the flavor I would swallow whole later. The bite of dry bitterness from your lights, red in the night, leaving. I cried that night, not for you but myself. I wasn't concerned about hurting you. Why would I be? I was so busy being concerned for myself that I didn't have time for you. *I did not have time for you.*

You came back again a few days later. You didn't want to be away from me. Why would you? You loved me so sincerely. A part of me, hidden deeply inside, wished you would have escaped when you had the chance. You were free, but instead of running to safety, you came back to try to protect me. Your efforts were in vain, and I wish now you would have used the energy to save yourself. I swam back to the present reality of despair.

My soul was on fire; not a creative inferno of passion, but a fire that was burning away at what was left of me. Completely possessed by the Serpent, I began to gasp for my last breath. Mercifully, finally, I would have the ability to take into me all of the tears that filled the sea in which I was about to drown. The pain I inflicted upon myself—my punishment for the pain I caused you—would be over after one deep breath.

The Serpent wrapped all its righteous tentacles around me. It pinned my arms back so I couldn't escape and my legs so I couldn't kick at It. I struggled against the nasty, slithery monster. I knew this was the thing I was here to witness. I wanted to leave so badly, draw in the breath that would allow me to sink into a quieter, softer hell. Let the fire eat me and the demons cut me. Let the most evil of beings tear me apart. It seemed like a reward compared to what I knew was on my horizon at the bottom of the sea. Surrounded by the broken hearts and my hair floating in tears, I prayed to a god I didn't believe in to allow me to embrace my death.

My head was being held so that I had to watch; my eyelids forced open. I then had to relive the day I finally did it. I finally finished my job, and absolutely, definitively killed you forever and ever, amen.

How you loved to make me laugh. When I would giggle, your eyes would positively light up. Even after all the times I had crushed your beautiful spirit, you still found joy in *my* joy. How could you have been such a dear soul while I continually chipped away at you? I wish it would have been possible for you to have been with a deserving mate. Oh, how you would have been cherished. Men like you are so scarce- brave, strong, kind, and generous. You may have been the last one of your kind, and yet I killed you anyway. What could you have become had you been appropriately loved? *I* loved you, and I am sure I love you still, if there is a part of me floating somewhere above this tear-filled watery tomb, but I didn't love you as I should have done. Such a miracle it would be if life gave us the opportunity to rewind, repair, and redeem.

You always did silly things during breakfast, even after the days of us touching knees had long since died and been left in the past. Your joy was contagious, even for a blackened, murderous soul like mine. You successfully juggled three sugar packets, and I clapped and laughed at your brilliant pride at the feat. You beamed and moved on to more significant items— bread rolls. One bounced and knocked my coffee cup over. Laughing, you came to my rescue with a towel. My shirt got splashed, and when you tried to dab at it, I became furious. I was going to kill you for coffee on my shirt. *For coffee on my shirt*. The selfish, shallow beast would not stay back. Instead, back inside I went to be replaced by the angry devil that had a permanent lease in my heart. Back deep, tucked away *behind* my heart and too far away for my arms to reach to try to pull the monster back again, I hid and quietly watched. I wanted to save you, but I couldn't reach, no matter how far I stretched.

I spat white-hot venom at you and could see it sizzle where it landed. Your face dropped to the floor as I knew it would. I had become an able assassin. I had been killing you for a very long time, and I always knew what to say to break you. Coffee on my shirt? How dare you. "I am so fucking sick of this constant messing around," I shouted an inch from your face. You backed up a step, and like a rabid animal, I came after you. I couldn't let you get away because you'd stained my shirt. You had been convicted and sentenced to death. I watched helplessly as the beast prepared the gallows.

You knew what was happening because you had been hunted by the monster before. You were such a brave man and so good. You would never fight back or stand up to me. Why would you? You cherished me. You would never want to say a cruel word to me, even to defend yourself from the jaws of the beast. You retreated to our room, where we shared so many life-defining moments, both happy and sad. You packed only one change of clothes and told me you would be back after I was calm, and we would discuss our future. You left, and I followed you to the door. My heart was sinking rapidly- *please don't go.*

I was scared now because you'd left before. Why did the monster always go away when you wanted to leave? I reached out to gently touch your elbow—a sweet gesture I had learned from you. You gave me a sad smile and told me it would be fine, and then you were gone.

A heated flash of fear shot through my body. It radiated from the center of my soul and spread equally throughout my small frame. The inside of my face was filled with heat; the same agitated anxiety one feels when speeding in a car and passing a patrolman. The heat you feel when a bad happening is imminent built up inside me. It took my breath, and I stood with my forehead pressed to the glass. I wished with all my might that you would return. I was terrified to be alone with the monster, and if you weren't here for it to feed on, it would undoubtedly turn to me for repast.

I stood at the window and watched your tail lights go down the driveway. Drizzling rain spitterspattered gently on the sill. Raw and rainy, it was a canvas painted perfectly for anguish. Your brake lights, dazzling in the splattering mist, came on, and I had a moment of hope, but then right-turn blinker...

The Serpent released me. The sound of sirens and whistles must have scared it, and it dropped me back into our empty living room at my position in front of the window. I was afraid to back away from the glass for fear of my thoughts breaking contact with you. I focused the energy of my chakras to a point in my head and tried to beam it to you and reel you back into the driveway. If I could only get you back here, I would find a way somehow to keep the monster far-flung.

I began to consider that the only way to stop the monster was to kill its host. If I let all of the blood out of me, it wouldn't be able to use my energy to harm you. Clawing at my wrists, trying to eradicate the horrible thing inside me, I lacked the courage required to decimate the wickedness that abided within. Too characterless, I was, to do this small task for you- it would have been one of the few unselfish acts of my life.

Why was I so weak? Why couldn't I protect you from the monster that lived in me?

Filled with profound sadness and worry, my thoughts were chaotic and frightening. Substantial dread made me unable to stand without leaning. A black cloak had been draped over me, and I became paralyzed with great fear for a very long time, and I sat; scared, shaking, and silent. The tears that soaked my shirt made me cold, but I savored them in my loneliness. Tears kept the beast away sometimes.

A knock on the door made me rise. Surely you would not knock. Why would you? You made this home for us with your love and strength. I answered the knock, thankful you were back. I was never going to allow this to happen again. I couldn't live without you, and I had finally realized what that meant as I'd watched your lights pulling away from me.

I pulled the door open to embrace you. But you it was not. It was never going to be you again. I had succeeded in killing you—and this time it was forever.

When I saw the uniform, I understood the sirens that had frightened away the Serpent earlier. A crash, they said, and you hadn't survived. *You didn't survive. Oh, my God. You- did-not-survive-please no-no-no.* I collapsed into the arms of the officer at our door. Sliding through those arms, I felt my face scrape against the zipper of his jacket as I slid out onto the stoop. My lip tingled with a slight abrasion from the policeman's coat. I was lying in the drizzle; the wetness familiar as I had just returned from the bottom of the sea. I gasped for breath—also a familiar feeling, and one so recent. A massive inhalation finally became possible, and then I screamed. My scream turned to a silent gasp for breath again, and The Uniform sat beside me. He placed a gentle hand on my back as I lay face down in the rain. My hands and arms were tucked beneath me, and my face lay on the wet cement. I was soaked wet, lying on the stoop with the policeman still softly holding my shoulder. He spoke to me gently, but the words tore through me like a sword. He got on one knee and tried to help me to mine. The grit from the cement stoop was stuck to my face, and I could feel it on my lips. He offered me a towel and a ride to the doctor. I declined his offer and sat on the stoop in the rain. The wooden bunny you whittled sat there with me. It peered at me with righteous condemnation from its little carved eye. "I'm so sorry, Bun Bun," I repeated over and over until my voice was gone.

The sweet policeman eventually left, and I sat alone, shuddering, crying, and vomiting. Clear mucus ran from my nose and mouth, and I couldn't even wipe it away. I thought for a moment about standing up from the stoop, but instead I lay back down on it, face first, and the grit stuck to me again. I kept my eyes open, and my lashes scraped the cement floor with my blinks. My nose was bent on its side from my head pushing it down, and I silently shuddered and cried more. The ability to take myself into the house and out of the rain was not within me. Rain continued to fall on my back, and each cold drop was a dagger. At times I thought of rising to go inside for comfort, but I wouldn't allow it. I *needed* to lay in the cold, hard reality of the rain since it dared to continue to fall even though you were dead. I lost all sense of time and, again, faded.

The grim Serpent swam away from me a few fathoms and turned around to watch as I struggled on the seafloor. Though no longer tethered by serpent tentacles, I still could not swim to the surface. The guilt and grief of the entire world would not allow me to rise. My Serpent grinned at me with a mouth full of jagged teeth. It motioned at me with a tentacle. It meant for me to follow, and we headed back farther into the dark abyss. I was no longer afraid, but hopeful that, soon, it would end my suffering.

I followed closely behind the Serpent as we worked our way around fragments of other souls that were unable to navigate the rocky seascape. Behind a pile of jagged broken heart pieces, the creature directed my vision to a hole in the floor of the gloomy sea. The blackness of the chasm was a stark contrast to the light brown sand mixed with bright red broken heart tatters, and the ambiance was surreal. I stood above it and looked in. I saw in that hole the day I had begun to die, because long before I killed you, somebody killed me. It was no coincidence that that was also the date the monster, dwelling inside me, had begun to awaken.

CHAPTER TWO:
SPRING FLOWERS DIE

Five years old, I was; with wispy yellow hair and a small, fragile frame. I was crying in the kitchen as Mommy and Daddy were fighting. I squeezed onto Mommy's leg as she tried to leave us behind. I put my small arm gently around her thigh. I didn't want her to go. Why would I? I couldn't care for myself and I needed her. Five-year-old children don't know how to be unselfish when their wellbeing is in question. One is born with no option other than to trust their caregiver for the essential ingredients required to survive and grow. If that responsibility is shirked, monsters begin to take over and provide nourishment. Hateful beasts seldom miss an opportunity to reside in an innocent soul- waiting until the time is right to feed on the energy of its host.

"Please don't leave me, Mommy," I cried. I didn't cry for attention. I cried because I was frightened. How would I get my vitamin from the "high up" cupboard? How would I have cereal when the milk was full and too heavy for my small arms to lift safely without spilling? Who would help me to brush the tangles from my hair? This couldn't happen. I couldn't be left behind. Fear flooded my tiny being as I begged to be saved from abandonment. Selfishly, I worried I might starve.

The moments were few in which I was held in the arms of either parent, but when the holding did happen, it fulfilled an inherent need that every living thing requires. With the absence of parental nurture, fanged demons willingly accept the role. The nurture of a fiend causes an innocent child to ripen into a hardened, harsh aberration that feeds on the hearts of those unfortunate enough to love it.

She spun around at me and shouted hot, hateful words. Then, with a diamond ring that was soon to lose its stone, she slashed her hand back through the air. The stone caught my tender eye, and it burned. The burning was not the lid or the side of the eye, but the gooey part; the *eye* part. Mommy and Daddy stopped fighting, and there was a drive to the doctor. I had to sleep there and have an operation. When I awoke, there were balloons and puddings, and so many faces happy to see me. Still, I couldn't see any of it. I had to keep both eyes covered until I was better, because if one moves, both move. A nice lady kept coming to my room and asking me if I remembered how I got hurt. I knew in my heart that I shouldn't tell. I shrugged and remained silent every time. I was so brave then. A small child required to use up all of the bravery allotted in the beginning only spells doom for the poor souls that intersect with the imperfect being later in life.

I was about to step into that hole to join my parents in a familiar place, but the Serpent, who seemed to be different—maybe even kind—now stopped me. I wanted to go since I had become exactly like they were. I had become a ring-slashing, eye-piercing monster, devoid of a human heart. If I were to jump into the abyss, I would finally be part of my family— the family who waited for me with open arms and snapping jaws. For a moment, I thought I saw a tear forming in Its eye. It waved at me, and I drifted away.

"Please don't set me adrift. I've followed you this far, and I have no one but you," I cried out to the beast who had now become my caregiver.

The Serpent reached for my hand, and I willingly gave it. Why was It gentle with me? Were we kindred? My feet dragged across the razor-sharp floor as It compelled me to come along. We walked along the lacerating ocean bottom, my feet being jagged by the debris of killed love until we came upon another hole. Initially, I began to leap into its bleak nothingness without a glance. Still, my friend held me near the edge and demanded I look inside. The heartbreak I viewed there caused me to step back. Who was the poor soul being tortured down there? She was so small. How could this happen to such a tiny child? I gazed into it and saw another instance when I was murdered slowly and cruelly.

Eight years old, and Mom and Dad were divorcing. We had to move to a new town, and I was frightened. With Daddy gone, who would take me to the hospital the next time Mommy accidentally slashed my eye or poked me with scissors creating a cut that needed to be sewn? Who would stop her when she put her hands around my throat until I couldn't breathe? I didn't want to live elsewhere. Why would I? I had friends and a school and a beautiful room to keep all of my cherished things. I could retreat into my special nook full of books and drawing paper. It was my favorite place. I could create my universe there, as well as read about worlds created by others in their beautiful stories.

I wrote my own stories in that nook. Unbelievable fantasies in which there were walks to the park, holding hands with a mommy and a daddy who wanted to share their love and play with buckets and plastic shovels in the sand. Fantasy tales of a foreign land I thought of every night as I drifted off to sleep; wishing on a star it would be real when I awoke.

"Please, Mommy, I am so scared. Can't we just stay here?" But she didn't answer, and she only turned to walk away. I walked behind her, and I reached out to hold her hand. I was so frightened. Why wouldn't I be? This was the only life I had known, and now we had to leave because of the yelling. I looked around for Daddy, because sometimes he had to rescue me when I touched Mommy when she didn't want me to, but he was already gone. I only ever saw him once more, but it was twenty years after this time. I needed him to save me *right now.*

She shook my hand away, spun around, and spat white-hot hateful words at me. I felt my face drop, and a silent scream tried to escape. Silent tears filled my eyes and dripped down my little cheeks. I had learned that, if I needed to cry, I must do so silently or there would be "something else to cry about." I was to shut up now and pack, or I wouldn't be taking *anything* with me. I ran back into my bedroom and slid under my bed to hide. A dusty sanctuary, I had eclipsed under there before. There was a monster in our house; not the kind that hides in your closet until you are asleep, but the type of ghoul that is supposed to give you love but can't.

My floor became wet from my tears as I silently sobbed. I didn't know the word "ally" then, but I knew I badly needed one. With all of my will and might, I clawed my way back out to the danger of the bedroom. I needed to pack as many things as possible. Mother said we were going to be very poor because Daddy had stopped loving us. I was so conflicted about what to bring and what to leave. I had been allowed three boxes to carry. I had to pack inside them all eight years of my life. No matter the dimensions of a box, it is very meager when one must insert the contents of their entire existence.

In the first box, I packed my most beautiful clothes and shoes. I rolled them up as small as I could so I could get as many as possible to fit. I sacrificed all of my ribbons and old play clothes because I needed to be as pretty as possible in my new school. One "jammies" and one "slippers" I took for comfort. I closed the lid but didn't put tape on it yet in case something needed changing. My small hands slid the box close to me so I could protect it.

The second box I filled with books. I tried to pick it up, but books are heavy. I was about to cry, but then decided to split all of them between my two remaining boxes so they could be carried. I couldn't leave without them. They were the only way I had to escape the scary parts of my life. Still too heavy, I tore the covers off of them. I loved the colorful pictures of fantastic things and the places they showed, but the words inside were more critical. Powerful words filled the pages and allowed me to visit places where horses ran wild and free, and houses were made of candy. Magical kingdoms existed where mommies and daddies spoke kind words to one another and cuddled their babies. There was no fear of slashing rings or stabbing scissors.

Mommy said whatever didn't fit into the boxes would be taken away by the garbage men who waited at our door with their big green truck full of discarded items from other people's broken homes. Choosing which of my beloved treasures to have placed in the smashing mouth of the big loud vehicle was the hardest decision of my already uphill life. Anguish and fear clouded my vision as I walked to exit the only safe haven I had ever known.

I walked out of my bedroom for the last time. It was the only place I had ever slept. I pulled the door closed behind me, reconsidered, and opened it halfway. One longing glance and I began to slide my boxes towards the uncertainty of the outside world and the car that was waiting to take me away. My shirt was soaked with tears. It clung to me like a bandage, and I savored the closeness.

The Serpent looked away from me, but not soon enough. I saw a tear form in its eye. It was a black tear that stood out from the red of the broken hearts lining the floor of the sea of heartbreak. It rolled down its face and splattered on top of the red debris littered at its feet. As I watched it sink and disappear, I wondered how I could be feeling dampness on my shirt while being under the teary water. Was I still wearing my tear-soaked shirt from the day Mommy made me leave my daddy, friends, and life behind?

My Serpent wrapped a tentacle around me. It was different this time, like a friend placing an arm around my shoulders. It began to walk, and I followed It to the next hole in the floor where I would watch the next time I was killed. Around this hole, beautiful daffodils grew and made a striking contrast to the red blood seascape. As I approached, they withered and died. Beautiful flowers cannot survive when they are planted in fear and sorrow. I stepped on the already decomposing blossoms- their white petals turning brown before my eyes- and carefully peeked into the horror of the pit's depths.

A frightened girl—me—was walking along a road in the dark. Her arms were wrapped around a box of books, with a dress and a doll balanced on top. Where was she going? She trudged along, her cries louder than the traffic speeding past. I peered closer and recognized her. It was nine-year-old me, and I was trying to find my way to my grandmother's house. I needed protection because Mommy was angry. Grammy always protected me when she knew I was in danger, but I wasn't permitted to call her for help. Since we moved into our new home without daddy, we were all alone and not allowed to seek solace in anyone—not even Grammy, who lived only a mile away.

I had spilled my drink and it had got on the carpet. I could see the blackened eye on my tiny face and the purple juice on my shirt. As I watched the poor soul bravely head for sanctuary, I could feel the swelling of her eye. I raised my hand to the injured place. The memory of Mommy picking my juice bottle from the floor flashed back to me with such rapidity that I nearly tumbled into the hole I peered into. Little me was shocked; I thought Mommy was picking it up to help me, but instead she used it as a weapon to hit my face. I could feel myself lying on the floor in the spilled purple nectar, unable to move. I needed to run for safety, but my face hurt so badly I was paralyzed.

I stood safely above the scene with my dear Serpent holding me firmly upright, and I watched as the mommy down below kicked the little girl as she lay on the floor. I vomited as I witnessed the weak, small thing claw for purchase on the carpet in a failed attempt at escape. I tried to jump in to save her when my tentacled friend spoke for the first time.

"She can't be saved. Only love could have saved her, but there was none."

I tried to jump in once again. Why wouldn't I? She was vulnerable and in extreme danger, with no prospect of help.

"You must only watch from above," It growled lowly into my ear.

I silently wept and watched as the kicks faded, and the mommy finally walked away. Witnessing the delicate baby eventually stand, wobble, and pack her precious things made me proud that I was her. I still had hope then. Traffic buzzed past, horns blared, and nobody stopped to help. I saw the car slow and pull onto the berm behind her—and, of course, it was the mommy. She grabbed the fragile me and threw her into the back of the car, leaving her beloved books, doll and dress lay on the side of the road. Escaping was not an option. Fortunately, my Serpent pulled me away so that I didn't have to witness what I lived through after Mommy took me back to her house.

The creature and I drifted across the sea bed. Numbness made it easier for me to flow with the current. The smell of my pain brought frightening creatures out of hiding, and they wanted a taste of me. How delicious my fear would be for them to devour. Their greedy eyes watched as I numbly floated along, still wishing I would die.

"Please, no more," I begged the slithery creature who had somehow become my only friend.

"More. Go, look at more. These are the reasons you are you," It said with what could only be sorrow.

I beheld another chapter of what became a series of killings to an innocent girl—a series that would eventually become what haunted her. In the early days of life, when I could have been so much more than the wretch I grew to be, I was destroyed.

There was a county fair in our new town, and I was old enough to go. The friend I made at my new school was coming with her parents to drive me there for a night I was so excited for that it filled my dreams every night for a week. I sorted through all my clothing, trying to find the perfect outfit for a special night of fun, snacks, and carnival rides. I finally decided on a new outfit my grandmother gave me, put it on, and excitedly went to the front door to wait for my friend and her kind family.

"You may *not* wear that. It's only for school," Mommy shouted. I turned to go change when my friend's car pulled into the drive. Conflicted, I touched the doorknob instead of returning to my room to change. White-hot fire numbed the side of my face from the blow struck by Mommy. I fell to the floor and watched her calmly walk out to tell the friendly people I wasn't feeling well and couldn't go along. When she came back inside the house, I tried to run away, but she caught me from behind and pulled me to the sewing room and shoved me to the floor. I watched in terror as she removed her scissors from the basket and began to cut my new clothes from me. Again, I tried to escape, and to stop me, Mommy poked them into my arm and used her other hand to hold me to the floor. The physical pain was bad, but the horror of watching my new outfit get shredded with scissors and violent rips was beyond words. I fainted, I think, and awoke in the darkened room with blood on the carpet, which I quickly tried to clean. Eventually, Mommy took me to a hospital to get the cut sown shut and told the beautiful nurse I was playing with scissors again.

Drops of blood mixed with the salty seawater as my Serpent embraced me. The wound from so long ago was open once again, and the predators were very interested in the source of the red nectar. My guide waved an appendage over the wound, and it quickly closed. I wanted to cry for the small, frightened me in that scene but realized it was of no use, so I bobbed along to view the scene of my next horror.

Friday nights, I was allowed ice cream. One scoop which had to be leveled off flat with a knife. Those occasions, I anticipated all week, counting down the days until I could savor the sweet vanilla cream melting and trickling down my throat. Most times, I would take it to my bedroom to enjoy it in quiet solitude so as not to disturb anyone with the sounds of licking the bowl.

Finally, my happiest day of the week arrived, and after my chores were complete, I rushed to get the bowl and scoop. I plopped the delightful treat in my special dish but forgot to level the excess from the top. Unfortunately, Mommy was watching, and she grabbed it from me and threw it against the wall. "You're greedy. Do you want us to starve because of your selfishness?" she shouted in my face. I knew the danger was close, so I ran to my room, turned out the lights, and tried to sleep.

I awoke on Saturday morning feeling guilty for my greed. I also felt relieved because I must have been forgiven since Mommy didn't come to my room and put her hands around my neck as she often did when she was angry, and I was sleeping. Cautiously, I climbed from my bed and softly walked to the kitchen. Mommy left a note that she had to go and would be back later. Being home alone was fun, and I was excited to have cereal in the living room while watching cartoons. My excitement turned to worry when I went to the cupboard and saw all the handles had thick plastic ties holding them closed. I tried to pull one off, but they were strong and wouldn't budge. The refrigerator also provided no help because it had been emptied and unplugged.

My only choice was to call Grammy for help. I was very hungry.

In the den where we kept the telephone, I was further dismayed when I saw the place where it hung on the wall was empty and just the wires hung in its place. I went back to the kitchen and drank water from the faucet and waited for Mommy to return.

Morning sun turned to dusk and then dark. Still, no Mommy and my hunger began to hurt. I searched the house for anything that looked edible. I remembered my Grammy once told me the little heart-shaped clovers that grew in the yard tasted like sour candy. "Sour Grass," she called them.

With great joy, I found our big silver flashlight and went to the yard to pick a feast. I filled my pockets with the little hearts and returned to the house to have a fancy dinner that I harvested with my own hands. *Mommy will be so proud, she will never have to worry about us starving again. I will pick clover every day and even save some for Winter when the snow covers the ground.*

I ate "sour grass" and drank water until finally, Mommy came home after two days. I saw her arms full of new clothes- for her, not me- and I realized there was something wrong with our life. I was much too young to have to come to this understanding, but come to it, I did. My mommy didn't love me. I was merely a rodent she was trapped with. My heart broke, and I went to bed silently and never got to tell her how I knew how to keep us fed with the "Sour Grass." *We* weren't poor and in danger of starving- *I* was.

I never tried again after that to love or be loved by her. There was something wrong with me that caused me to be unlovable. Most of my quiet time, I contemplated what that thing might be. I decided I must have been born wrong, evil, greedy, and unnecessary. Six long years passed before I felt vanilla ice cream melting in my throat again. It made me cry when I finally tasted it after such a long time.

From my place kneeling on the seafloor, my insides ached from what would have been hunger in a life where sustenance mattered. At my side, partially buried in crumbled heart sand, lay a bowl brimming with wilted, brown "sour grass" and a rusted ice cream scoop. I shoved them away from me and went to my Serpent so I could follow it to the next act of this macabre documentary of my life.

Sixteen years old and a job I had! Freedom and an old car that became my sanctuary. I went to school and straight to work every day, and on the weekends too. The restaurant was fun, and I had friends there. I was so happy to have a place to go and money for clothes. After work one day, I stayed to talk to friends and have a snack. I looked at the time, and I realized it was late, and I had to go. Scary heat rose through me. I was going to be late getting home. I drove so very fast and only made it because the angels didn't want me to die so quickly. They wanted me to be killed slowly by hateful words, shattered glass, and cold air.

I arrived home ten minutes later than expected to find the door was locked. I knocked, but there was no answer. The lights were out, and darkness made it impossible to see inside. I was freezing and wanted my bed. Shivers became shakes, and my fingers were so cold. My nose was frozen, too, and it began to run. I felt panic and then a teary eye. It was a school night, and I slept in my car, shivering because I didn't want to use my gasoline to have the engine make heat.

Mother came out in the morning and pounded on the window. Shouting from her made my cold ears ache as she yelled, "You're no fucking good." I could feel the air change with her anger and become poisonous to breathe. Even through all the turmoil of my young life, I was shocked by her words. Holding my breath, covering my face, and waiting for the worst to pass, had been a natural part of my life since I was small. This felt worse, though, and I was more frightened than ever. I was no fucking good. *I was no fucking good.*

I *was* good, though. I was *very* good. I worked so hard to achieve good grades and I worked a job and earned my own money for clothes. Did Mommy have to say I was *no fucking good*? Of course she did;

somebody had killed her once, too. That is what happens. When somebody kills you, you must kill somebody else, and forever and ever on it goes.

A rock smashed my window. I cried because I was scared. Do mothers break their children's windows with stones? Of course they do. It was happening right then and there. I slid onto the floor and protected my cold face from the smashed window. Mother saw my tears and screamed at the broken glass.

"I hate you! Leave and don't come back," she shouted. Her words were sharper than the shards of my broken window. I flinched from the cuts they made as I pulled shattered window glass from my hair. Where would I go?

I quickly drove away and hid my car with the broken windshield in the woods by a stream with a frozen, glassy top. I was so frightened. January was cold where we lived, and I had no clothes for school other than the ones from work. I slept in my car under blankets I made from the rug in the trunk. I sipped the drink I had left from work the night before, and I waited to die in the cold. Sixteen I was, with no place to go. The sounds in the forest are deafening at night when you are sixteen with a broken-windowed car to sleep in and nobody to care for you. Snaps of twigs are the monsters that lurk in the darkness. Owls are demons, and the wind is a scream.

The Serpent walked away from me, and I tried to call out to It, but no sound came from my mouth. You can't make sounds when you are under teary water. I was alone in the sea now, and I was getting cold. The current became sharp, and broken pieces of hearts swirled around my head. Their jagged edges scraped my face. My eyes stung from the dust made from the souls of those who kill and become killed. I braced myself against the strong current and hoped this would be the end. My hair swirled up above my head, and I heard a tortured soul calling to me. It was asking me to come toward its voice, but its sound was swirling all around me.

"Who are you?" I needed to know. Silence. I picked up the shell of a broken heart and held it to my ear. It is said that you can hear the sounds of every hurtful word ever spoken in the shell of a broken heart found on the seafloor.

The voice inside asked if I could forgive. I didn't understand. In an effort to make the sound clearer, I shook the shell in hopes dirt would sprinkle out. If I could hear, I could possibly understand what I must do so that I could simply inhale all of the tears of the world into my lungs and drown.

"Are you ready to forgive?" the voice asked again, this time softly.

"Forgive who?" I asked. The shell was silent, and so I shook it and asked again, "Forgive who?" The sounds I heard from holding the broken heart shell to my ear only sighed. If I had to ask, then I was not ready.

I was swimming in scary solitude now in the sea of heartbreak. It was challenging to move, but move I did. I was so alone there, and my only companions were the souls of the heartbroken that floated above me and wailed. While I swam, I noticed a doorway with a large keyhole. I approached and peered in. Sadness overwhelmed me at the poor young girl I saw through the slot. She was alone and afraid. As I started to look for a way to open the door and help her, she turned to face me. Her tear-streaked face and the lines of her frowning mouth looked familiar. She was me, and I began to understand. I saw yet another time I had been killed.

Spring flowers turned into summer swelter. The grass was dry and brown; the life baked out of it. I strolled around the yard of my mother's house, mourning the loss of my grandmother. I hadn't been to this house since the windshield-breaking and door locking of three years ago. Nobody was home. The rest of the family was at the funeral home, making arrangements for my dear Grammy. I was at the rear of the yard when they arrived. I could hear soft tears and gentle words. I craved both of those things with a pang of raw, powerful hunger. I had been starved and I longed for just a nibble of the love the members of my family were sharing. One is never so alone as when they are on the outside of love and comfort with no way in. I craved even an icy dagger from a family member. I wished I could join Grammy in Heaven, where we could play card games and eat colorful hard candy.

Afraid to enter the house, I paced the yard. Remembering the hard days of solitude, I resumed my isolation. My energy focused on trying to wish somebody to come from inside to where I was and perhaps offer me a bit of comfort, but that comfort didn't come. What happened instead was a mother yelling out of the window to either get in or leave. My sorrow grew heavy, and I collapsed on the lawn in tears. Clippings from the freshly mowed lawn stuck to my face as I lay face down on the ground breathing the sweet grass. I heard the door slam and angry rantings cross the yard. I got to my knees and waited for the bad stuff.

"Get out of here. You are not wanted. Things are hard enough without your need for drama. There are things more significant than you," my mother shouted. She raised a foot as if to kick me but stopped as I went limp before her.

I began to crawl until I found my feet and ran to my car. I sped away so as not to incur another broken window. My driving only lasted a moment, and I had to pull off the road because my tears made me blind. As I sat, crying silently, I heard a car pull off behind me. I was afraid to look. As long as I couldn't see, I would still be able to cling to the hope that mother had come to embrace me and take me to her home so I could mourn the loss of Grammy with my family whom I hadn't seen in so long. But my mother, it was not. It was an uncle, and he told me it would be better if I kept going until I was out of sight of the visitors of my mother's home. I was upsetting the guests, he explained.

This final interaction killed me. I died. The innocent, hopeful me was gone with the harsh words and burnt grass.

I dreamt of someone who would love me completely, and then I met you—and you did just that. I killed you for it.

Sorrow will follow me all the days of my life.

CHAPTER THREE:
DEATH'S HORSELESS
CARRIAGE

When my mind finished its wandering journey to revisit the death of an innocent girl, I returned to the grief at hand. With the policeman gone, I managed to get indoors. My heart was aching so badly I wanted to die. I tried to drink water, but my hands shook so violently that I couldn't get the glass to my gritty lips without spilling. I had a moment of clarity and calm, and undressed for the shower.

I was freezing and soaked, my clothes made wet *sploot* sounds when I peeled them off and dropped them to the floor. I turned the hot water on in the shower and waited in front of the mirror until it warmed. I stared into the mirror at my face, trying to make sense of the person looking back at me. It was strange, I was still here, still had a reflection, but the part of me that I cherished was dead. *You.* I felt so sad for the wretched black soul in that mirror that I thought briefly about killing her, too; after all, killing was my specialty. The moment, as dark and stormy as it was, nonetheless rendered me paralyzed and unable to take the action required to put the monster to death. The handful of pills fell from my fingers and to the floor. Where did they come from? I didn't even remember opening the bottle.

I turned from the steamy mirror and entered the hot tomb of the shower. All of your products were in there—a half-bottle of shave cream and a razor that would never need the blade changed again. Your shampoo bottle stood almost empty. What would become of it? No one had ever used that shampoo but you, and now you were gone. I began to think about all of the unfinished things left behind. What would become of all the items waiting for you? I put my back against the shower wall and slid down to sit on the floor. I screamed and held my wet face in my trembling hands, rocking in the shower and shaking from the intensity of my cry. The steady patter of the shower water hit all over and around me. Head down between my knees and sobbing, I began to feel faint.

I cried until I passed out, presumably from a lack of oxygen, and was greeted by my Serpent. We stood together now, on the floor of the sea of despair. There was no longer a need to restrain me. I *wanted* to be there. It was lovelier in the saline tomb than alone with my thoughts in our home, which was now devoid of all hope of your return.

I regained enough of myself to shut off the now-cold shower and half-heartedly towel dry my trembling body. I walked—naked and alone—to our... *my*... bedroom, where I found the T-shirt you wore when you used to be alive. I put it on, hugged it to me, and, of course, I wept.

As I paced the room with no idea where my steps would take me, I opened your dresser drawers. I think I hoped to find something inside of them to make me hate you. Perhaps there was a nasty secret you had ensconced that would reveal how rational and reasonable I had been for treating you so poorly. Instead, I found a pencil eraser in the shape of a bunny. It was a gift I had given to you after you had crafted the wooden one sitting outside, seething hatred at me for destroying you—its giver of life. I hadn't seen it since the day I'd brought it home and put it in your Pop-Tart box as a gag. You'd chosen to keep it in a secret place; it was the only thing you had hidden away. I placed it on my pinky and continued to amble about aimlessly. My legs grew heavy, and I could pace no more.

Bleak, thick, profound sadness encircled me. It stank of rotten fruit and singed hair, and I couldn't get away from it. I took some clumsy steps towards the bed just a few feet away. My legs were leaden, and the sadness became so thick I felt as though I were wading upstream against a powerful current. I dropped myself to the floor, having made it only to the rug near our bed. I lay there, pulling the side of the carpet around me to use as an itchy blanket. I slept, I think, albeit for just a moment, and when I regained consciousness, I gazed under our bed.

I found a book you had been reading. Page two-hundred eighty-eight you had been on, and you used a playing card—a ten of clubs—to mark your page. I placed a scrap of paper in between your pages, and took the floppy, thinly worn, ragged card. I carried it around, holding it to my face. It was nearly as soft as a tissue. I placed it against my nose to try to get even a slight fragment of your scent. I carried it to our basement, where you had a room for playing games. On the end-table was an unfinished beer. I picked up the bottle and touched the mouth hole to my lips, trying to breathe it in. I carried both the bottle and the card with me, the bunny eraser still peering about from the heights of my pinky.

Back up the stairs in the kitchen, I protectively held my treasures. I sat at our table, placed the physical memories down in front of me, and made a circle around them with my arms. I stared and tried to focus all of my energy on them. I tried to communicate with the prizes you had left behind, to send a message to whatever remained of your DNA that may have been attached to them even in the smallest way. *I am so very sorry, and I genuinely love you,* was the thought I tried to deliver. I focused my thoughts entirely on those sad little items. I wished, in that moment, that alchemy was real. If it were, I would cast a spell to bring you back; make a new *you* from the tragic gifts I had gathered, and hold you for eternity, never again speaking any words besides, "I love you."

I begged God to make a precious miracle for me, but God said to me through my thoughts, "I already did, but you killed him."

I begged further, sincerely asking him to take me in your place, to bring you back. *Why is it impossible? Could you not do it if you wanted to? Of course you could, you are God.* How I wished it would have been me instead. You'd had so many gifts you could have given to the world. All I had left was an empty black soul, a playing card, a beer bottle, and a wooden bunny who sat outside the door hating me.

I made my way to the sofa, where I held the remnants of your life. I sat there for an unknown amount of time. Time stopped passing in a linear format, with eternity consisting of a loop in hell ahead of me—a loop in which I am still stuck to this day.

The morning of your funeral, it was. I hadn't slept. I dozed a bit from the pills prescribed by a doctor, but the sound of your voice in this empty house was deafening. When my eyes would close, I would hear you, and it would jolt me awake again, almost like a shout in the darkness. I arose in the night and took to pacing the floors. Every step creaked like an old man's bones. I leaned against a wall, and it reminded me of how it felt when I would lean on you and felt you pressing back against me to hold me up. It caused me to think of how I would turn around and place my face into your chest, breathing in the smell of you.

I made toast and took it to the couch to eat. I took a bite and immediately tried to count how many slices of toast I'd had on this couch while we were in the *touching knees* stage of us. I dropped it to the floor, and once again cried.

My face felt so heavy that it became hard for me to close my mouth. The tender flesh under my jaw tingled like an appendage that has partially lost circulation, and my breath became labored. How could I even begin to do this? How could I go to watch you be placed under the ground forever? My tears were always right at the corners of my eyes and ready to gush at any moment. Once again, I begged God to please bring you back and take me away. Once again, God spoke back, telling me, "You do not deserve to be removed from the pain which you have created."

I had a beautiful black dress to wear to your funeral. Putting it on my weak, shaking body was surreal. I had to wear it for you because you died. Because I killed you.

I began to apply make-up, and I thought of how you would stand behind me in the mirror and smile as I made the necessary faces to apply the required products. I cried and had to begin again. I did the best I could without the mirror because I could not look into it without seeing your reflection directly behind me. A black ribbon I used to tie my hair. You loved it when I wore ribbons. You said it made me look like a cartoon doll.

A car came to take me to where the preacher would say words about you, and then another vehicle would take you to where they would stick you in a hole, and I would never see you again. I wished I could be numb like everyone else was. I can't be comfortably numb with shock and grief.

I stumbled out to the black, long car, and a kind man opened the back door for me. When he closed the door, it made a dull thud. The sound made me weep. It was such a fitting sound; final and cold, and closed off from everything. The car began to roll forward and picked up speed as we went down the street where we shared much of our lives until you died. I watched out the window, amazed at how everything in the world continued to move along. How could it? You were gone. As I watched out of the side window of the long black car, we passed a towing garage. There sat your smashed car, and I screamed for the kind man to stop. He quickly pulled off of the road, and I had the door opened and was out crossing the street before he could stop me.

I went over and pulled on the door to open it, but it wouldn't budge. Stuck tight, it was like a warped barn door. The window was broken, so I stuck my head inside. Oh, the blood was everywhere, and so thick in places. Bits of broken things stuck in it and some were smeared onto the dash. The bag with the single change of clothes you had taken was strewn on the passenger floor, and everything was wet from the rain that had seeped in through the hole they had cut in the roof to get you out. They must have thought they could save you, but they could not. You were dead. I scooped up shards of broken glass from your seat and cradled them in my hands. Your blood, still stuck to them, had turned dry. I squeezed the beautiful jewels tightly, and my own blood mingled with yours. I began to scrape at my wrist with them. If I could get our blood to mix, then perhaps I would die and become one with you. It was my only hope. If I could slice my wrists right here, at the side of your car, the last place in which you had been alive, quite possibly I could see the sunshine again. How quickly the sun slides below the horizon when our lives have shattered into pieces of broken windshields, crumpled metal, and ripped blood-covered seats.

The kind man from the funeral car came to me and gently pulled me back from the wreckage. I turned to him and placed my face onto his shoulder while I shuddered and wept. He gently pried the shards of broken glass from my hand; they fell to the ground, and I yearned for them. Our bloody reunion smeared on the driver's lapel as I clung to him for life. I started to stumble, and he caught me. My driver hero put his jacket on the ground and helped me to sit down beside the smashed car in which you had died. Eventually, he helped me up. He never spoke, but somehow he knew the time was as right as it ever could be. With his arm around me and his jacket over my shoulders, he took me back to the funeral car.

The asphalt made my shoes click and clack loudly. You would have laughed because you always laughed at the sound of my clacking shoes. You referred to it as my rain dance. I loved you for that reference. Cherished were the things that only you would think to say. How could I live without ever hearing one of your quips again?

The compassionate gentleman held my arm as I stumbled into the church. My knees were so weak I couldn't hold myself up. My heels—which I always wore so elegantly—clicked and clacked down the aisle. They were very loud against the somber, silent room. I wobbled to my seat in the very front, hearing gentle sobbing in the pew beside me. I didn't have to look to know it was your parents. I wished so badly I could trade places with you. I would love to give you back to them. You were so loved by everyone you touched, while I was just a black-hearted killer of souls whose own parents didn't even arrive to hold me up in that festival of grief. No phone call, no note, not even a flower to lay upon your box and fill the air with the honeysuckle scent of death, was provided by them.

Sweet words were spoken of you, but they were not enough to convey your real beauty. Sobs came from around the small church as speakers spoke and weepers wept. The sounds of sniffles echoed across the high ceiling and down around my head. I tried to shoo them away, but they were mine, and as people were leaving the church, I remained by your side.

A car waited for me, but I couldn't go. I stood beside your box and gazed upon you. I put my hands on the side of your coffin and tried to make myself touch you, but I was afraid. I wanted one last touch; to brush your face with my hand. I reached for you but stopped myself. I wouldn't be able to touch you for the last time. How could I? I never prepared myself for the final touch. I never knew that killing you would make you actually die. I thought I could keep killing and touching you forever. At some point in every life we touch and are touched by our love for the final time, but most of us never know which time is the last. If I had known, would I have let go? Of course I wouldn't have. Just because I killed you did not mean I didn't love you.

Something soft touched my back. It was your mother's kind hand. She whispered to me and kissed my cheek. She told me it was time to go, and gently pulled me back from your box. When my hands lost contact with it, I cried until I couldn't see. Your beautiful mother led me out of the church and to the car that would take me to the hole you would be in forever.

The interior of the vehicle was surreal, and everything was plush and red. The car started to move, and with the movement my consciousness began to fade. I struggled to stay alert and to observe the scenery as I had wanted. I could store it away for eternity and bring it back to the front of my thoughts whenever I wished. Everything was gray and cold. Your mother's hand remained on my knee for the entire ride. She was so strong and brave and had enough love to comfort me, the beast who tortured her baby to death. I felt the car slow, turn, and finally stop. My breath escaped me, and I became rigid and terrified. Seeing your body carried inside of a box to be placed in a hole was not something I had realized would happen until the very moment we stopped driving.

"Come on, sweetheart. We will stand together," your sweet Mommy said to me. How could she? I was a monster that didn't deserve compassion. Surely she knew I was the reason her boy was going to be underground forever. Why be kind to me?

We walked to the side of your grave and listened to more words, more tears, more sobs. Ashes and dust turned to mud and drizzle as the rain began to quicken. Somebody held an umbrella over me, but I couldn't look back to see who. If I looked away, it would cost precious seconds—seconds which I could instead use to stare at your coffin. I stared in silence until all the words were spoken, and the men began to lower you into the ground with velvet ropes.

"No, no, no, no," I whimpered and fell to my knees in the sticky mud beside your freshly dug grave. My dress clung to me like wet papier-mâché, and I reached for the handle as it sank out of sight. I lay there in the quicksand, vomiting and wailing for what must have been a million moments in an endless circuit of eternal hell.

Eventually, I made my way to our house and sat in dark comatose silence for what felt like an eternity that flashed by in a second. People came to check on me, but I didn't answer the door. Darkness was my solace, and I was unwilling to allow any light to enter my sanctuary. Days turned to nights, and then to weeks and months. I sat alone and silent except for the sounds of my cries and pleas to a deity to either return you or take me, instead of leaving me here to suffer.

I would doze for minutes at a time, and in my dreams you were alive and here. Your car stopped at the end of the driveway. The flash of brake lights was your return to me, and I cherished you for the rest of our lives. We sang, danced, laughed, and drank the dew from leaves in the forest. But every time I would awaken from a dreamy doze, I would be confronted with the agony of your passing as if it were new once again.

The pain of waking from my dream was too intense, and so I tried to stave off sleep by cutting my flesh with your razor. The pain would keep me awake for a little while. When that no longer worked, I began to contemplate cutting my neck open with it instead. If I were in a permanent state of sleep, perhaps my dreams of you would also be lasting.

I filled our bathtub with warm water and slid inside. My hand shook with fear as well as malnutrition as I hadn't eaten in several days, and as I began to slice, I saw your face—and it cried. I slept then, dreamless and sound, until the chill of the water woke me.

CHAPTER FOUR:
THE FOREST OF DESPAIR

After an indeterminable amount of days, months, or perhaps years, I had a moment of clarity. I had been in a transcendent-like state, reliving my entire life like an extended sad dream. As I rambled through the home I shared with you, my deep grief gave way to self-loathing and despair. On the bathroom vanity, I found the pills a doctor had prescribed to calm me after your death. I poured them into my hand and swallowed them all. A lethal dose it was not. Was a deadly dose my intention? Perhaps. In a moment, I fell to the floor only to be awakened by a familiar voice I could not put a face to.

"Walk toward the forest," it commanded me. It was a decree I ignored. Deep sleep overtook me again, and I had troubled dreams of serpents, wrecked automobiles, and hate-filled bunnies staring upon me with condemnation. My sleep came and left in waves, but never went far enough away for me to rise out of bed. I could only see shades of gray, and the door to the outside was such a long distance away it could not be walked.

I awoke again days later with a ravenousness that caused me to tremble. Stumbling to our kitchen to search for food, I saw my reflection in the beautiful mirror that hung in our hallway. I remembered the day we hung it. We had stood embracing one another in its shimmery reproduction of us, but now I gazed at the gauntness of my face and the dark circles under my eyes. Behind me was your ghost. You looked worried, and I turned to face you, but of course you weren't there. My moment of hopefulness that I could embrace your spirit dissolved into greater agony. I dragged myself to the kitchen and found an open box of crackers, which I poured onto the table.

Though stale and salty, I nibbled at the edges of those that were still whole. Aged crackers are hard to swallow, especially with a dry mouth. With a full glass of water, I broke the saltines into pill-sized bits and choked them down. I knew I must take in nourishment, even though I had no desire to remain among the living. Amazingly, I began to feel a bit of energy flow into my wasted body and decided to shower. I slipped out of the clothes I had been wearing in my comatose state for weeks, and let the hot water run over my head until it became cold. The remnants of mud, still tight and masking my skin from your funeral, left a residue at the bottom of the shower. I wiped it with a towel and carried it with me to our bed. I crawled under the blankets and cuddled the damp, dirty towel next to me and slept. The dreams returned and, eventually, so did the familiar voice.

"Walk toward the forest," it was an order, and this time I contemplated heeding.

Slowly, I crawled to the edge of the mattress and carefully placed my feet on the floor. Back in our lovely kitchen where you juggled sugar packets and dinner rolls, I scraped the remaining crackers from the table into a paper bag. I filled a jar with water from the faucet and walked outside for the first time since I had watched your coffin be lowered into the cold dark hole scooped out just for you.

My bare feet slapped on the cement porch where, a million years before, I had lay crying in the rain with grit stuck to my grief-streaked face. I picked up the wooden bunny you had carved for my pleasure and, with my cracker crumbs and water jar, I took it and began to walk through our back yard, not knowing where I was headed. A force had summoned me to a place of which I had no knowledge. Compelled by it, I followed.

Thoughts did not exist at the front of my consciousness. Driven by some power from outside me, I walked in a straight line. I crossed lawns, passed over driveways and through puddles and streams. I could not stop my legs from moving in a direction that seemed to be determined by something outside of myself. As dusk settled, I entered the forest where we had once held hands and skipped on the pine needles in our bare feet. My arm brushed the tree where our initials were carved with a heart hugging them together. Numb, I stopped to stare at the hieroglyph made with love from your soul. A tear trickled from my eye and down to my lips, and I drank it as if it were dew from the tree of life. I savored the salty tear, and when it dissolved, I put my head down and walked on toward whatever fate lay before me in the forest of despair.

Dusk became darkness. The silence of the forest was deafening and surreal. Was I truly there, stumbling aimlessly through a dark landscape that smelled of sadness and curdled dreams? As the blackness of the wooded world blended with the darkness of my soul, I screamed from agony of loss. When I cried, I cried for you, but when I screamed, it was for me. I thought one scream would make it better, releasing the feeling of dread and gloom, but once it escaped me, I could not stop. My cries turned to shrieks, which turned to silence as all of my breath was gone, and I fell. At first, I fell only to my knees. As I knelt on the soft leaves, yet another scream escaped. Strange was the only thought I had, which was, "Where do I put my hands while I shriek?" I fixed them to the sides of my face, and their location enabled me to scream at a higher volume. With my air gone again, I fell forward, onto my face, and lay on the ground shuddering, near convulsion. All remaining light had gone, and I lost what remained of my consciousness.

A voice caused me to stir. At first, I thought, perhaps it was you. I jumped to my feet to run to you, climb upon you with a fierce embrace and never release you. My heart leapt, my pulse quickened, and I had never experienced such great joy in my life. Never in all generations would there ever be anyone who would be kinder and gentler to anyone as I would be to you. I received redemption and a chance to change the unchangeable. But you, it was not. My wooden friend, Bun Bun, was standing before me. Not long ago, I had been terrified of the whittled being. It hated me for killing your dear soul, of course it did, but now I was thankful for it. It had softened and become kind to me.

"Where am I, Bun Bun?" I asked. "What am I doing? What is the purpose of this?"

The Bunny turned and began to walk deeper into the forest of despair without a word. I followed. I did not want to be left alone.

My companion glided like a ghost through the dense forest, and I lost sight of it. I called out for a pause, but it kept moving deeper into the unknown. Once again, I was alone to stumble through the thick sadness of decay. The path was dark as it winded through green moss and brown, dead leaves. Twisted branches pulled at my clothing as if they were trying to turn me around and send me back to hell.

I walked deeper into the sorrowful woodland. Days I walked without rest or repast. I became excruciatingly thirsty and dropped to my knees at a trickling stream. As I bent to scoop water with my jar, I saw the reflection of a tortured soul. The soul was mine, and was identical to the souls that lay crushed on the ocean floor, where I had trampled before. Behind me, there was yet another reflection, the image of my rabbit friend. It appeared weakened and thirsty, in need of care.

I took my handful of water to it so it could drink, but instead it waved a modest paw over me, and I slept and dreamed.

Walking hand in hand, we were in a hurry. There were storm clouds and lightning, and I was scared. You picked me up from the ground and carried me to a tree that overlooked a field. The tree was odd and had an aire of wisdom, and the field contained tall plants that swayed, golden in the breeze. You spoke to me in that dream. I believed it was indeed your voice coming to me from wherever you go when your beloved kills you with fiery words of nastiness and hurt. Your words quenched my thirst and removed the worst of my pain.

"This is the Tree of Forgiveness. You must seek it, climb it, and then you can look out upon the Field of Light. You will find me there. The way to redemption is in the branches of the tree. Do this that I ask of you in honor of me."

"But, my love, I do not want forgiveness. I was a horrid monster, and I need to live out my time running through this dark dream," I sobbed into the dream-void where I thought you were. Hope turned to despair once I began to awaken. Realizing it was an illusion, I wept again, just as I had on the day I lost you. Perhaps my eternal punishment would be reliving the loss of you, the heart of my heart, every single day for the rest of time.

"Why?" I screamed into the forest. The echo was the answer. Why, indeed? Why? Why did I allow you to leave that day? It would have been so simple to cling to you, to beg your forgiveness, to behave kindly, to use sweet words of love for the rest of our lives. Any single, simple act by me would have saved you, and not just on your final day of life but on any day since first we had met.

As I lay on a dirt path in the shadow of the Bunny, all my misdeeds continued to play out in front of me on a screen made of pine boughs draping over the soiled trail. The theater of hopelessness gave me a front-row seat. I watched in agony, all the things I have ever done or said, that were less than what true love calls for. Would my torture ever cease?

"The Tree of Forgiveness will let you be free," the Bunny stated, responding to my thoughts.

Since there did not appear to be any other way, I stood and fumbled my way along the path that I reasoned must lead me to the tree I had been commanded to seek. My bare feet quickly became covered in soil as I walked fast enough so that I would not lose sight of the Bunny who seemed to know the way. Seemingly, an eternity passed, and still I tramped across the path, deeper and deeper into the dark forest. Time became immeasurable, but after many miles traveled, I came upon jagged rocks that reached so high up into the trees that the tops could not be seen. I stopped and marveled at their magnificence. There was a perfectly flat stone in front of them, and I sat upon it, looking for the Bunny in hopes it would share the moment with me. I heard thunder before seeing the lightning.

It was a strange land, and so I wasn't surprised that storms didn't follow the traditional rules of nature. The glow of the electrical storm caused the Bunny to become illuminated and remain so even after the flash.

"These rocks are for you. Do you see the tops?"

"No. I only see the bottom. How can I see what you want me to see?" I asked my wooden guide.

"You cannot see the peaks with your eyes. A forgiving heart is required to view the majestic summits. Can you forgive?"

"But I don't understand who to forgive, my dear friend. What must I do? I want to see the glory of the rocky pyramids," I said to the Bunny. "I wish to dive from them into the hard ground here at the bottom."

"Still, I say, if you must ask, you are not ready," the Bunny said, and floated out of my sight. I didn't want to lose it because it was created by you, my love, with the aim of bringing me happiness and laughter, but my focus was still on the odd rocks before me. Desire to know what was at the top consumed me, and I desperately needed to find a way to comply with whatever was being requested of me, but still I was confused.

Dense fog swirled around me, and I entered a state that was becoming familiar. My sleep brought visions that both comforted and disturbed me, and I was no longer able to determine if I was awake or asleep. The short dreams in which you spoke to me became my only source of hope. If I could eternally walk through this forest of despair and have capsulated dreams in which I could hear your voice, I would consider myself blessed. The brief, muddled sounds of you became everything. The dark clouds seemed lessened when I was able to hear your phantom calls. My dreams and reality mingled.

I could see you. You were a young boy playing with a ball in an open field. Your beloved dog from your childhood was with you, and you glowed. Toss after toss, the brown pup would retrieve the ball and bring it to you, and you would laugh. Your happy laughter cleared the fog, and it lifted away like a funnel cloud. The vision of you inspired me to rise and walk on to find the tree in hopes I would understand what forgiveness was being required of me. I walked on in the dusky light that remained from the Bunny's glow.

Not long after I began to trek again, I saw a woman's figure on the path. I had not seen or spoken to this person since I was a frightened child, and approaching her caused me to feel anxious. Was she friendly? Was she lost? Was she a nasty thing with gnashing, sharp teeth?

I paused to think, and saw her beckon for me to go to her. She wore robes that flowed down her body and were so long the bottoms lay in the dirt on the path to the Tree of Forgiveness. The brown earth that stuck to the train of them was a stark contrast to the bright white cloth of which they were made. Her long, frazzled silver hair was familiar to me, and I became frightened because the familiarity felt dangerous. I cautiously approached, and she reached out to me with a gnarled, boney hand. I didn't want to get closer, but was somehow unable to resist the pull of her. I wished for the Bunny to come to my rescue, but it did not. I was alone now with the being I feared most.

My mother, wrapped in her white robes, was dead and standing before me. Her decayed hands protruded from the cuffs of her dress, and I could see in them every object she ever used to strike me. A scream caught in my throat, and I struggled for breath. Years spent longing for her while simultaneously trying to escape her culminated in a meeting in the Forest of Despair. I tried to run away, perhaps find my way out of this terrifying forest and return to our house. If I could make it back home, I could use your razor to slice my neck and release my tortured soul from my ragged body. Alas, my feet would not move. They were bound to the roots of a gnarled tree, and my mother appeared to be in command of it. She waved her hand of bone at the tree, and its grip tightened.

"My daughter, I have been waiting for you here for eternity. Why are you frightened of me? I am a dead thing and cannot harm you." She spoke, and her words chilled me.

"Mommy, you harmed me with no remorse throughout my life. I'm here looking for my love who died because I damaged him just as you damaged me."

Her outstretched arms filled me with fear, and I put my hands to my face for protection. I felt her dead, boney arms embrace me, and I waited for the pain that would come. Instead of pain, I felt her firm embrace, and then her gentle release as she stepped back from me.

"Is it you, Mommy, that I must forgive so I may see what is at the top of those strange rocks?" I asked.

I saw a teardrop made of dust fall from her sunken face and vanish in the breeze. She waved her arms over my head, and I entered a state of knowing. I watched what I had suspected all along: somebody had killed her long before she had ever killed me. The killing is a continuous loop, I realized.

My mother, as a young girl, was a strange concept for me to grasp, but she stood before me as I was in the doorway of her childhood bedroom. Loud footsteps banged up the stairs and approached from behind me as my grandfather burst through the door. He was drunk and shouting. My mommy scrambled to put objects between herself and my furious grandfather. She ran around her small bed and became trapped between it and the wall. She wasn't quick enough to get away, and my grandpa, whom I so loved, punched her in her belly. I watched the fear grow on her face as she lay on the floor, trying to cover her vital parts from serious injury. He kicked her while she was down, and her screams reminded me of my own. My grandpa pushed my mommy's dresser over on top of her and left the room, his weak daughter alone and hurt on the floor.

"Why did he do that, Mommy?" I asked, shocked. I never saw my grandpa be anything but gentle, and part of me feared this was a trick being played on me by my evil mother.

"He did that to me because his father did it to him. Once the violent demon takes residence in a family, it stays with them for all of eternity—unless, that is, someone is strong enough to break the chain. I was not, you see. Are you, daughter, strong enough to break the demon's back?" she asked, and waited with her arms folded in front of her as if she still was trying to protect herself.

"No, Mommy, I'm not strong enough," I said, before asking again, "Is it you that I must forgive?"

"I desire your forgiveness, but it is not me who you must forgive, daughter," she said, and I detected a quiet sob escape her throat. Dry and raspy, the cry sounded like the groan of the wooden stairs in the home she took me away from when I was small.

"Then who, Mommy? Please help me. I'm lost in this forest, and I need help."

"There were many times I could have helped you and wished I would have been strong enough, but I cannot help you now. It is forbidden. If you must ask who, then you are not ready. Follow the path to the tree. Once you find it, look for the Field of Light. You will see your beloved there, and it will be up to you to decide if you can touch him again. Nobody can walk the path for you. You must walk it alone until you reach the end. I love you, daughter. I always have." And then she was gone.

As she faded away from me, I ran to the spot where she had last stood. I wanted to embrace her once more. I didn't know she had been beaten and abused. I had lived in fear of her and found it unfathomable that she could ever have been a victim. I believed her to be the maker of victims, not the victimized.

The roots that bound my feet loosened, and I continued on my quest. I had to keep looking over my shoulder to make sure my mother wasn't following me. I was still frightened and untrusting of her. In my back, it was almost like I could feel every evil thing that ever existed staring their burning eyes through me- approaching me with stealth. I began to walk faster because I expected that, at any moment, a hand made of bone and knife would land upon my shoulder.

A breeze began to blow, and on it wafted the scent of an aftershave that reminded me of someone. I couldn't identify who, exactly, but it was an old memory. As I walked around a corner, I saw him standing in the path. Daddy.

"Daddy, what are you doing here? I haven't seen you in so long. You promised to visit me after the divorce, but I never saw you again. Why did you forget me? I needed you," I said. My anger subsided and turned to sadness as my father cried in the middle of the path. "Mommy hurt me many, many times, and you weren't there to protect me." I took a step toward him. I wanted to embrace my father, but my hands drifted through him as if he was made of the fog that seemed to fill the forest.

Finally, he spoke. "Many times, I should have come to you. I knew your danger, but I was weak. I float here now, and I *can* save you from what awaits if you continue to seek the tree. Turn and go home. Abandon this quest and find a life that will be sad, but where hope exists. Those who guide you are not your friends. They are wicked, vengeful things. The true Field of Light you seek is back in your empty home that still can be full of love—someday. If you continue, all hope is lost."

"Daddy, I *must* go to the tree. My love waits for me in that field that is only visible from the branches. The Bunny told me so."

My father's fog evaporated and he was gone once again—just as he had been the times I had needed him most. I lifted my chin, and boldly walked forward until sleep overtook me. I dreamed a familiar dream from a happier time.

I walked with my father, hand in hand, in a field filled with green clover. Barely tall enough to reach his hand, he picked me up and carried me on his shoulders as I laughed and squealed. From my elevated view, the lush emerald-colored shamrocks stretched as far as I could see and were punctuated by tall purple flowers. I was frightened of the bees as they busily went about their chores, and my daddy comforted me and told me the bees were our friends. The idea of having so many bee friends buzzing to and fro filled me with supreme happiness, and I giggled every time one came near.

"Shh, be very quiet and look where I'm pointing," Daddy whispered the words to me. I followed his finger to a brown spot way out in front of where we walked. "That's a deer eating the delicious clover. Let's see how close it will allow us to get."

"Daddy, we shouldn't try to get close, it's enjoying its snack. Can we watch from here until it's full?" I said with great hope.

"My, you are such a caring child. Others would want to run to it and laugh when it scampered away in fear. You're good all the way through." *I was good all the way through.*

Those words carried me through many of the hard, scary years after he left us. I dreamed that dream often when I was small, and savored the kindness. Oh, if he had not left me alone with Mommy. What could I have become? No matter- I was fully awake and had a journey in front of me.

With the realization I must now trek alone to find the tree that seemed to hold the answers I sought, I began to move along the trail through the Forest of Despair. I traveled by foot for a very long time, powered by visions, both frightening and enlightening. I wondered if anyone back in the real world in which I used to reside had realized I had been gone for a lifetime. I briefly closed my eyes and saw the plants in our empty home, which had already begun to wilt, turn brown and die. Our bedroom window was still open. I left it open for you, my love, in the chance that your spirit might find a way in and lay with me. The curtain billowed in the breeze like it used to when we left the window cracked open on the hot summer nights. The curtain would blow in and tickle me sometimes. My giggles would awaken you, and we would lay and talk for hours. Long undisturbed, a small spider made a web under the ceiling fan and patiently waited for a treat. Dust covered the dresser top, and the shower faucet continued to drip. How could these things still go on without us?

I see our mirror. The tall, odd rocks from earlier in my journey are reflected in there. I see the tops of them now in the shimmery silver mirror. I couldn't see the summit before because I was too close, but now I have stepped back, and everything is visible to me. I had to find the tree. It would lead me to you.

CHAPTER FIVE:
THE TREE OF
FORGIVENESS

I journeyed onward while thinking of my mommy. I mourned for the time we could have shared had there not been a history of killing whose beginning was untraceable. I wept for her, for me, for my grandpa and, most of all, for you, my love. I thought of my daddy. Was I selfish to wish he would have stayed with us, even though that wasn't where his heart took him? Would I have had protection, or would he have stopped loving and caring for me just as he had for my mommy? I didn't weep for him, but for myself and my deprival of a family so many of my friends had and enjoyed.

Could a better start to life for *me* have saved *you*, my love?

The landscape of the forest began to change. Trees were not as close together, and rocks became a more common sight. Moss grew on them and provided an interesting green contrast to the dark, gloomy forest that had become my home. I began to struggle to remember our house outside of this odd place, but I didn't forget your face. Every blink of my eyes showed me your smile and drove me onward into the unknown. My heart swelled with the hope of finding you standing, waiting for me, in the field of light.

In the strange complexity of this world, I never grew hungry or thirsty. I abandoned my cracker crumbs and jar of water on a rock near where I visited with my mother. With every step, I became more and more aware of a light so far off in the distance that it had to be unreachable by foot. Whatever was guiding me was taking me toward the luminescence, and I was both frightened and excited by it. I could sense the calling of the Tree of

Forgiveness and hoped I could figure out who or what I was to forgive so I could move forward with— or put an end to—my life. The unending sorrow was worse than death, and I yearned for a terminus.

In the distance, I saw butterflies fluttering about across the path. It seemed as though a million lifetimes had passed since last I saw one of the winged beings. I went to them with great care so as not to harm them. I remembered very well how fragile they were, and I could not bear to cause any harm to the happy little bugs. I didn't seem to be getting closer to them, and I badly wanted to be in their company, so I began to jog in their direction. Nonetheless, no matter how fast I went, the distance didn't close. It dawned on me that they were leading me where they wanted me to go, and realization dawned that I had left the path. Only a few trees remained in my vision as I followed the fluttery beings, fully trusting them to take me where I was meant to be.

Soon I saw them near a tree. The pretty bugs waited for me while fluttering happily about as they rode the breeze that blew in from the source of the light. The tree had long, twisted, knotty branches on its gigantic trunk, and it made for an eerie landscape, but I was not afraid to approach. The sky was stormy and calm all at the same time, and its hue was the dark purple of an eerie haunted place. At the moment I was close enough to touch the ancient wildwood, the butterflies vanished. I leaned on the rough bark and considered where I should go now that I abandoned the path to follow the wispy wings of the beautiful creatures.

"Climb as you did when you were a child," a voice whispered on the breeze. The suggestion retook me to a happier time where I would climb trees in the yard of my childhood home, and sometimes pick a bouquet of leaves for my mommy to put in a jar of water on the table. On extraordinary adventures, acorns would be stuck to the small branches, and I kept them in a cup hidden under the porch- a pirate's treasure I would check on regularly.

I stepped back to look for a way to climb the tree and saw two figures sitting high in its limbs. My only two friends were perched there: the Bunny and my dear Serpent. I pulled myself hand over hand up the limbs until I reached them, and sat between them as if we were a life-long group of close friends. I was comfortable in the tree, and we all sat quietly for a very long time. I looked around from my wooden throne and could still see the prominent light I had been following for the latter part of my journey. The incandescence appeared different from the lofty height of the tree. It seemed more like its own entity than a commodity to illuminate the world we were sitting in. I couldn't bear the silence any longer.

"Am I in the Tree of Forgiveness?" I asked my question without directing it to either of my guides roosted in the gnarled branches beside me.

"You are in it, is it in you?" The Serpent was the first to speak.

"I simply do not understand. I have traveled through seas of heartbreak, rode in cars that took me to places of mourning, and met with my deepest fears along the way. My heart is broken, and I am weary. Will you please help me?" I begged and glanced back and forth between my two mysterious guides.

"This is where you must see and decide. We will be here to help you, but only after you have learned the purpose of your journey," the Bunny said without looking at me.

"Bun Bun, I'm so sorry for killing your maker. Will you please forgive me? Is this enchanted tree for me to earn *your* forgiveness?" I began to weep out of fear that my Bun Bun still hated me.

"I am but a carving of wood. The spirit of me is what you seek, not my forgiveness," the Bunny said, and the words felt cold and harsh. How could the Bunny be so obtuse after everything that had transpired? I turned to my Serpent.

"Am I here to forgive you for holding me nearly lifeless on the floor of the Sea of Heartbreak? I do forgive you. I understood why I needed to be detained there and punished for my evil deeds." I pleaded for answers.

"I'm not to forgive or be forgiven. I am but your own will and a symbol of your desire to die. Why did you not die in the sea? If you find the answer to that question, you will find the answer to everything," the Serpent said. I was unable to tell if the Serpent's tone was sad or simply uncaring.

I began to think about my journey from the time I was a fragile child until this very moment, as I sat in a tree with two parts of two souls; one yours and the other mine. I spent so much time since your death thinking about what you could have become if I had not inflicted word wounds upon your precious soul. I wished you would have found someone other than me to love, even though loving you was the highest honor of my life. I neglected to consider what I could have been to you—and, more importantly, what I could have been to myself. What if I had not become afflicted with hurtful words and violent attacks from my mother and abandoned by my father to face her wrath? The answer then came to me.

"I must decide whether or not to forgive myself to move beyond this tree and enter the field of light." It wasn't a question. "Or return the way I came and go home."

My two friends nodded silently.

"I don't want to. Forgiving what I have done would be wrong and disrespectful to my love," I told them. "If I decide to not forgive, I will stay in this crooked tree forever- not returning home or entering the field where my love awaits."

"Now that you know the answer, it is time to choose. That is why we are still with you. Your journey will either continue onward or end," the Serpent told me, and the Bunny nodded in agreement.

"Please help me decide. How do I know what to do? I don't want to walk away from my love and go on with my life. More days of dark, dreary sadness, I cannot endure. I want to go to The Field of Light and be with my love. How do I know which to decide to take me there? I want to go there even if it is only for a moment to beg forgiveness and tell of my never-ending love for him?" Forgiving myself is not an option, there must be another way." I tried to move; I wanted to escape the tree and find a way to the field without meeting the requirements. I would walk until the end of time if I had to. I could not move, though. I was paralyzed in the tree.

The Bunny waved a paw over my eyes, and I fell into a trance. I forgave myself for the things I did wrong. In my dreamlike state, I had a vision.

Climbing out of the tree, I walked for a short while and returned home. Things were just as they were when I left as though only moments had passed. I mourned for many years and eventually lived happily but with numbness all the days of my life.

My life became normalized; I found a new love in time and had a family of my own. I married a kind man that was not you, my love. We had a wispy haired daughter who spilled juice and came home late.

But I could not relax and enjoy our life. I remained fearful of the monster that would always dwell in me would attack my family at any moment. I was too weakened to fight it forever, and if I killed them with harsh words or misdeeds, they would either die or go on to kill others. My days were filled with panic and fear of becoming to my child what my mother had grown to be to me. Days at the park with my new love that was *not* you were full of anxiety. At any moment, the beast within me could push the true me aside and chew on the family I was supposed to love. If I went to them in the way my vision suggested, eventually, one would be tragically killed, and the other would be alone in The Forest of Despair with demons and bunnies to have as companions. This was not an acceptable outcome, and I shook the vision away.

I arrived back in the tree with my guides, and the Serpent waved a tentacled appendage before my eyes. I fell once again to my trace. I did not climb down from the tree but leapt. When I landed, I found myself in the Field of Light. I looked around and saw you throwing an orange ball to a big brown dog. You were laughing, and cast a ray of pure joy. I ran to you, held you, and told you all the things I thought you needed to know. I was finally out of the blackness and could amend the wrongs I had created with my nasty words. I held one of your hands as the other tossed the ball. We laughed together in the field and remained there, happily ever after.

Once again, we would walk hand in hand, and I would never let you go. While we would never be able to return to our beautiful home, we could frolic in the Field of Light; you, your beloved dog, and me. I saw us grow old together, laughing still at your slobbery dog chasing his orange ball. The sun would never set on our lives. Never would it drop below the horizon.

My decision was made, and I kissed the Bunny and told it goodbye. I was going the way of the Serpent. The Field of light was where I needed to be. The Bunny floated away, but I saw it glance over its shoulder; its wooden eyes full of tears. Just the

Serpent and I remained in the tree, and it moved closer to me. I held its snake-like arm to my chest in an embrace, then wrapped it around my neck; tugging to be sure it would not loosen.

CHAPTER SIX:
BOUGHS BREAK

And now I stand here on this branch with my face warmed by the sun. I am not afraid but relieved. The breeze is comforting, and the air smells sweet. In a moment, all of the wrongs will be right, and the pain will be extinct. Soon, the voices that have been screaming in my head will be silent, and I will join you in the beautiful field. When I arrive, my love, I will remain next to you and supply all of the comfort and enjoyment you deserve. A harsh word will never be uttered from my lips ever again. Finally, I will kill the wicked thing that has lived in me since I was a small child. Finally, I can be the one to protect *you*.

I see you there, my love; playing with your dog and laughing. You are looking around the field. Can you feel me? Soon, very soon, I will be at your side. We will have not a care in the world. Light, airy happiness will replace the vest of lead, and the monster living inside me will cease to exist. You will receive the whole, complete, loving, me that you deserve—that you *always* deserved.

"Do not do it, my child," Mother is saying to me from above ~~me~~. She is standing atop the mountainous rocky pyramids which I was so enamored with inside the forest. Where they her rocks? Dead leaves are falling from where she stands, and I watch them flutter past me and land softly on the ground below. Dead butterflies swirl past me and mix with the dead leaves at the trunk of the tree. She is here to take away my chance of happiness just as she had done for my entire life. I would not allow it- I am no longer frightened of her.

I look at her, then quickly look back to the field where happiness and peace exist and are too powerful to allow darkness to reside. I step closer to the edge. With my back to her, I say, "This is the desire of my heart. Why, after all the cruel things you have done to me, would you want me to remain in agony? Why would you deny me my happiness?"

"I have already jumped from that branch. The Field of Light isn't what it seems. It is an illusion designed to lure you in, but the light is a false one." My mother's words create a moment of doubt in me, so I begin to move quickly before my cowardice prevents me from finding you and being eternally happy.

I feel The Serpent's arm tighten around my neck. It reassures me and makes me feel safe. I take yet another step closer to the edge and hear my mother cry, and so I turn to face her. Her robes are gone, and she is but a skeleton with dusty tears dripping from the sockets that should hold her eyes; eyes easily deflated by shards of glass that fall from rings of broken promises.

"Do not listen to her. She has already taken her leap from the branch. Do you think she has your best interests in her rotted heart? Did she ever?" my Serpent asks.

I am trying to listen to both of them, but the noise is too much. Now, with a trembling body, I pull the tentacle securely around my neck. Nothing matters to me except getting to you in the field. Already, I can smell your skin, and the scent assures me this is the only thing to do. I hear the wails of my mother as I calmly step off the branch.

Through my fall, I see the events of my former life. My mother and father are in the delivery room as a small child is handed to them. They look so happy and share an embrace, careful not to crush the gift they are given. I feel my mommy's heartbeat as the doctor lays me on her. I see a tear of joy in my daddy's eye. A moment of pure love I never knew had ever existed or passed between them.

I see my first day of school and the friend I had—until I killed you and lost myself in the crash. I watch as we trade snacks from our bags, which had obviously been packed with great care. We play games on the sidewalk with colorful chalk and have sleepovers. We eat snacks and stay up too late until our giggles wake the grown-ups who send us to bed, laughing all the way.

I am falling now past my sixth birthday party. Grammy and Mommy are playing with me and laughing at the silly birthday hat I crafted out of milk jugs and crayons. My friends are playing games outside, but I want to be with Mommy and Grammy. There is a bright light shining on us all. I want to stop here, but the journey of my fall continues.

I am walking into a banquet hall for a reception, and all of the chairs are taken—all but one that is vacant beside a handsome boy that is you, my love. I find out you chased your friend out of the chair, so I had no choice but to sit next to you. I am sitting beside you now in the remaining chair, and you are saying silly things that make me giggle, and I cover my mouth. I am instantly in love with you. We get up to dance, and you hold me close. Please let me stop here. I want to live in this moment with you. I reach my arms to try to catch something to hold me there. *Please keep me here.*

As my fall continues, I see so many happy times I had forgotten ever existed. I want to stop at each one and visit. I reach out for each moment as I speed by, wishing to embrace the good things that should have been good enough to vanquish the evil creature that lived within me. No matter, I am on my way to you now, my love. I see the Field of Light approaching, and I brace for that delicious impact.

CHAPTER SEVEN:
THE FIELD OF LIGHT

I gently land in the Field of Light, and find myself walking toward the sound of your laughter. I see you and begin to run in your direction. You are throwing an orange ball to your beloved dog. I remember you showing me pictures of him from when you were a boy. Happiness fills my heart, and I plop on the ground to watch and not interrupt. I will never be selfish again. Never will I spoil another moment for you. I am so pleased to have the opportunity to now be to you what I always should have been.

You don't see me at first, and I enjoy watching you experience perpetual bliss. The dog sees me first and comes to greet me. When you see me, you wave and rush to my side. I embrace you so fiercely and kiss your face, covering every inch of your skin.

"My love, I'm so deeply sorry for the things I said to you when we were alive. Never again will I utter hurtful words to you. I have learned so much and know the cause of my destructive behavior. Please go back to playing with your dog. I want nothing other than to watch you," I say through tears of complete joy.

You scratch your dog's ears and sit beside me in the grass. We watch in silence as your pup runs amok in the field, chasing butterflies and barking at the breeze. I lean on you, and you put your arms around me. I have missed your smell and the feel of your warmth so much since you died. All the horror was worthwhile as now I get to be here with you; here with you in the knowledge of how it would be without you.

The Field of Light is a strange place. It seems odd there is nobody here but you and your dog. Where is everyone? I want to ask, but since you are yet to speak, I think perhaps you wish to enjoy the silence. Since your every want is now my only wish, I simply remain at your side watching your pup scamper about. You grab my shoulders and gently turn me toward you. We sit now, face to face. Why do you look sad?

"I already knew the reasons why you said the things you did. I love you because I knew that those moments were not you speaking. I knew from the first time the monster appeared when we made the static shock in your apartment that you were infected by a nasty beast. Please know that I never thought poorly of you," you say to me, and the sound of your voice warms me all the way through to my soul. But still I wonder why you look so sad.

"I'm here now, my love, and I'll never hurt you again. I have dreamed of being near you since I watched your tail lights flicker at the bottom of the driveway the last day we were together," I softly tell him.

"But you are hurting me now. Can't you see?" you ask so sincerely.

"Oh, no. What have I done? I will fix it this instant. Do you want me to give you time with your doggy? I will wait here and watch for all eternity. I'm never leaving this field. The only thing I want to do for the rest of forever is to be next to you, to smell you, touch you, and hear your laughter," I plead.

"I sent Bun Bun with you to show you the way to peace. You learned so much about yourself and had such a wonderful life ahead of you. You can't stay here forever. You will have to leave soon."

"I don't understand," I weep. "You said you forgive me. I promise I'll never be nasty again. Please let me stay. Why don't you want me to?" I sob. "I can't leave. I don't know the way home from here, and I won't go without you anyway."

I become aware of a clock hanging on the horizon. Nothing is holding it up, and it is odd and ominous. It must count down the moments in which I am permitted to stay with you. I want to waste no more time with words, and I know you do not wish to either. I lean my head on you and sit quietly. The clock is alive and running fast. I have just a moment left to say once more, "My heart of my heart, I love you. Please forgive every wrong: it was a monster living in me."

"I do forgive you. In fact, there is nothing to forgive. I know all the reasons for everything you ever said and did. The Field of Light is not a real place. The only real place was back to our home, where you could have mourned and then started anew. I'm so sorry, but the time has come for you to leave. Please leave knowing I loved you and accepted you—*and* the monsters that tore you to bits. I wish I could have fought them away. I wish I could fight the one away that is coming to take you. Please just look at me now, then close your eyes and count to ten like we used to do when we would play childish hiding games in our yard."

I do as my love requests and become frightened to find that this place is not real. What will happen to me? "One, Two, Three..."And my eyes close, I have a dream.

In my dream, I climb to the craggy tops of the rocks of my earlier vision. My parents await me, and

I walk to them. I see every wound ever inflicted upon them when they were as innocent as I once was. Full understanding comes to me, and I mourn now for the life they could have had if they would have been handled with love instead of neglect and nasty words. We join hands and dive from the cliffs into the rough, hard ground below. The poison of us will go no further, infect no others, and it ends with us.

"Seven, Eight, Nine..."

When I reach ten, I open my eyes, and the light has been replaced by dusk, and you are gone.

I stand and begin to walk in hopes of finding a way back to the light when the Serpent appears. It motions to me just as it has before, and when I follow, I find myself back in the Sea of Heartbreak. We bob along the bottom, and once again my feet scrape on the fragments of broken hearts. My Serpent guides me to a hole in the floor. This one was wider and somehow different than the ones he kept me from leaping into when we were last here. I walk to the edge and peer in. Confused, I turn to the Serpent for direction.

"I don't understand. There is nothing in there. No tormented souls or horrifying scenes. Just blackness. What is this?"

"It is for you."

Immediately I understand. I walk to the edge and finally step into the silence I have been seeking since the pain of the way you were taken from me overtook my lost, black soul. As I fall, there are no happy memories. I pass by tortured beings, screaming and writhing in pain. I pass a funeral and find that it is for me. Your Mommy and Daddy are there, and I watch as they lay a flower on my casket. There is a picture of me on a table, and people whom I care for but have neglected in my despair are weeping. Our house sits empty, and the lawn is growing high. Our garden that we planted with pride was brown and dead. People come to start removing the remnants of our life that have been left behind.

A child picks the bunny from the stoop and runs with it, laughing.

I cannot tell where this fall ends. I know the end will not be a soft landing in a light-filled field. There is no light here, only hurt and darkness. Perhaps this is the end I have been seeking, but it seems to be such a waste. No matter, I will cling to the last I saw of you; playing with your dog in the beautiful field.

I hope the end of my existence brings awareness of how dangerous words can be if they are shot from a cannon, rather than gently laid on a pillow of feathers, ready to share with your love.

CHAPTER EIGHT: A WORLD OF HOPE

Words contain immense power. It is possible for a weapon used in anger to misfire or lose its way to the intended mark. When words are used as weapons, they are deadly accurate and cannot be placed back in a holster once they have been released.

Cruelty tends to get passed along from generation to generation without anyone knowing the reasons why. Monsters lurk in each of us. They weaken us to a breaking point, and unfortunate consequences arise. In a moment of raw emotion, keeping your words holstered is difficult. Still, please be aware: they are incredibly hurtful when used without care. A harmful phrase fired at someone out of anger not only kills a part of the person who is on the receiving end, but also kills a portion of the one who does the shooting. After a time, it becomes more relaxed and more comfortable to fire words with anger and hate. While the pain may begin to feel like it is numbing, the bruises still appear. Unlike a common injury, verbal bruises never fully heal, and the continued addition of new ones compound on top of the old, and eventually, all involved become crippled.

At some point in everyone's life, you speak to a loved one for the final time. We don't usually have the luxury of knowing when that time will be. Would you want the last words you say to a loved one be cruel ones intended to harm? Of course, you wouldn't. You are a kind and good person. You can't erase the hurtful things said to you in your past, but you can try to honor them by being kind in the future. The scars of words from your past cause you to scar others in your present.

You never know what another person has endured or are presently enduring. It takes a great effort to be mindful and to speak kindly. There will be slip-ups along the way. Learn from them and remember that repairing immediate damage is much easier than trying to excavate word shrapnel out of scar tissue. Try your best to live in the present moment, for that is truly the only moment we can control. It is a most challenging task—remaining present. (I still fail at it regularly- keep trying) The peace you derive from successfully completing it, though? It is true peace that cannot be found through riches or things. The present moment is all that any of us, rich or poor, truly own. Simply, it is all there is; the only tangible item that exists.

Finally, there is help for depression and anxiety. These conditions don't suggest you are weak; they mean you are hurt. It takes a brave soul to seek advice. There is not one person who has not experienced some form of horror, neglect, abuse, or profound sadness in their life. Anyone who looks down upon another with judgment for seeking out care for their mental health has also been wounded. They cannot help it; they have a monster devouring their soul. They just have not yet been awakened to the fact that a problem exists. Hope always exists even when it is impossible to believe. One never knows what might happen in the next ten minutes that could be the most beautiful life-changing thing imaginable.

If someone you know is hurting, reach a gentle hand out to them. Don't judge or offer advice unless asked. Be there, be present, and be compassionate. Compassion is quite possibly the most significant power we have against dangerous creatures that lurk in our hearts and devour the happiness of those we love.

Please always follow the path of the bunny, for it was carved from love. The Serpent may seem like your friend—but a friend it is not. It will push you into the abyss from which there is no return.

I leave you now with the comfort of Rumi. Seek him.

> *Come, Come, Whoever You Are*
> *Wanderer, worshiper, lover of leaving.*
> *It doesn't matter.*
> *Ours is not a caravan of despair.*
> *Come, even if you have broken your vows*
> *a thousand times*
> *Come, yet again, come, come.*

—Jalaluddin Rumi

ACKNOWLEDGMENTS

K. Bennett: I think tonight about our drive through the desert and across the country heading to our destiny as I type the last sentences of this work. Your undying support of all I do is the greatest gift possible for one to give another. Your kindness and compassion for the weakened is an inspiration.

P. DeSanto: Thank you for the adventures, they saved my soul. Here's to many, many more.

Tina Lewis: You are a treasure. From the bottom of my heart, I say if it weren't for you, I would not be drawing meaningful breath today. Your ability to be kind while calling me out on my bullshit is a once in a lifetime talent. May all the peace in the world be with you always.

E. Rubenstein: Your courage through personal tragedy has been an inspiration to me. You have played a significant part in expanding my mind, and I admire you greatly.

Dr. S. Deckert- Finally, somebody taught me how the hell to properly end a paragraph. Thank you for that and your honest and kind critiques.

Hayley Paige: Thank you for giving my book your loving care and laying your talented hands on this, the work of my life. It has been a heart-wrenching journey, and I'm happy you took it with me.

V. Levin: My favorite artist in the world. How you can pull an image from my mind and turn it into a book cover is magic.

The Family I Have Been Fortunate Enough To Marry Into: I am grateful to and appreciative of you all. Thank you for accepting me even while I have spent so much time absent from everything.

Grammy: I miss you and hope someday I find you in The Field of Light. You protected me when I was unable to protect myself.

Finally, Mom and Dad: Most likely, neither of you will ever be aware this book exists, but of course, it wouldn't exist if not for you. I refrain from telling you about it because I don't want to cause you pain or guilt- we've all had our fill of those ingredients. We had a tight hand dealt to us. Forgiveness and redemption come in many textures, and we all deserve every layer. I wish you to have peace and happiness, and I hope your lives are fulfilling in whatever way you want them to be. I love you both and wish your struggles would have never come. With that said, please know this: I understand.